The
Dark Side

Stephen Campana

World Castle Publishing, LLC
Pensacola, Florida
Copyright © Stephen Campana
Paperback ISBN: 9781629894287
eBook ISBN: 9781629894294
First Edition World Castle Publishing, LLC, February 29, 2016
http://www.worldcastlepublishing.com

Licensing Notes

Cover: Karen Fuller
Editor: Eric Johnston

Noted Quotes by other authors are marked in the novel and used with their permissions. The authors are: Richard Smith, Stephen Matthies, Peter Bradford Martin, and David Hume.

To my brother.

"The only God whose existence I cannot disprove is the one who disguises his every move as something else."

— Peter Bradford Martin

Chapter 1

The further Nick drove, the worse he felt. He was driving *into* something. Something bad. Some kind of storm, but not one consisting of a mix of moisture and unstable air. No, this was far worse, a singular force and exquisite malevolence.

As a pastor, he was not unacquainted with evil. He had felt it before, but never anything like this. Never anything close. On the scale of evil — with one being a black cat and five being an army of vampires — this was a three, and building rapidly the closer they came to their destination. His hands were clammy, and beads of sweat ran down his chest as his pulse quickened and his breathing labored to the verge of a full-on anxiety attack. He needed to get a grip, and already he was fidgeting in his seat, unable to sit still, playing with his collar, massaging the steering wheel, rubbing his chin — anything to keep from staying still and feeling the full force of the dread that was welling up inside of him.

He looked over at Willie, embarrassed. He was supposed to be the cool one. After all, this was his job. He was a demon hunter. He and Willie traveled the countryside searching for demonic activity. Then he drove it away, while Willie—the cameraman—captured it all on film for broadcast on a cable show called *Into the Devil's Den*. That was the gig, and they'd been at it, as a team, for seven years now.

Thing was, he never felt this way before his other confrontations with evil. In fact, he no longer even believed he was actually doing battle with demonic forces. Just the equally malignant, but far less sexy, forces of mental illness and superstition. Tonight was challenging that belief big time. He did not feel like he was driving into a deep, dark pit of superstition. Or mental illness. No, this felt like something different entirely.

He looked over at Willie. "Something tells me the ratings for this one are gonna be great," he said, trying to lighten the mood.

"Something tells me you're right."

Ratings. That's what it was all about now. Oh, at first he believed he was really helping people battle their literal demons. But no more. Now it was all about getting some good, blood-chilling stuff on film and sending it in to the studio, where they would edit it, then air it on a Friday night cable show called *"Into the Devil's Den,"* which featured himself, Pastor Nick Gallo, battling real live straight-from-the-pit-of-hell-demons. And beating them! Sure, he didn't believe it anymore, but what was he supposed to do? Just call in sick one day and say, "Sorry, but I don't believe in demons anymore"? He couldn't do that. And besides, the work he did really seemed to help people. What difference did it make if it was psychosomatic? Wasn't all illness, at bottom, the work of Satan?

Of course it was. He looked over at Willie again. "I think we're close," he said.

"How can you tell?" Willie asked.

Nick wanted to say: *Because the sense of palpable evil that's been swelling in my gut for the last ten minutes just shot up about six notches.* Instead he said: "I can just feel it, that's all."

"You feel it, too?" Willie asked.

Willie felt it, too. Nick didn't know whether that was a good thing or a bad thing. Good or bad, there was no turning back now. Although he felt like it. He felt like simply turning the car around and speeding out of there as fast as four wheels could take them. In fact, if they didn't find the place soon, that's exactly what he would do. He would have to. His nerves would not hold out much longer.

"I think you need to make a right," Willie said, pointing to the GPS mounted to the dash.

He looked at it as the arrow starting widening, and a serene, gentle woman's voice said, "In twenty yards, turn right."

Nick didn't know whether to feel relieved or disappointed. He was kind of hoping they *wouldn't* find the place. He leaned forward, squinting to read the street sign. Yep, that was it. That was the street they were looking for — Blackwood Clemington Road. He made the right and started down the road, driving slowly so they could read the numbers on the houses. "Damn," Willie said, "even the street name sounds creepy. Blackwood."

Nick forced a smile. Willie was right. It was a creepy name.   Blackwood.   Blaaackwood. BLAAAAAAACKWOOD!

Clemington.

Road.

Creepy all the way through. He craned his neck,

looking for the number 442. That was the address — 442 Blackwood Clemington Road. The houses on this street were small and old and ill-kept. Some were barely more than shacks. The lawns weren't much better — overgrown with grass and untrimmed shrubbery. Many of them didn't even have any lights on, and it was only 9 PM. Even the ones that did showed no signs of life. No pedestrians on the sidewalk; no kids on the porch; no dogs on the lawns. Nothing. Just two rows of drooping old houses on a dark, desolate, dead street.

After a minute or so, Nick miraculously managed to make out one of the house numbers: 394. That meant the house would be on his side of the road, just a few doors up. As it turned out, it was the last house on his side of the street. Last house on the left, Nick thought. He was pretty sure that was the name of a horror movie. The thought did not comfort him.

He pulled up in front of the house. Parking was not an issue on this street. He looked at the house. Except for a faint stream of light shining through a large front window, the house was as dark as night. It looked like something out of a horror move: old and dark and dilapidated, with peeling paint, broken window shutters, and cracked wooden siding covering walls that literally sagged beneath the weight of a busted up roof and a crooked chimney. The place looked like one strong wind could just blow it down.

Nick took a deep breath and looked down at the open notepad on the console. He picked it up and read the notes. It was a typical assignment. An old man, John Cockers, was, in the opinion of his family, possessed by a demon. The family consisted of his wife, a grown son who lived there, and a ten-year-old grandson who had been placed in the home while his mother battled alcoholism.

Nick shut the car off. He looked over at Willie. "You ready?" he asked. Willie took a deep breath, looking like he wanted to answer no. Instead he said "Let's do it." The two men got out of the car and made their way to the front door. The porch creaked slightly beneath them. Thick layers of green moss covered the railings. Above them hung a broken light fixture, ensconced in cobwebs, with exposed wires snaking out the sides. The cobwebs also filled the corners of the windows sills and the door. Beneath their feet lie a cruddy welcome mat with the word *Welcome* almost too faded to read. On the middle of the mat, belly up, lay a big, dead, desiccated cockroach.

"Lovely place," Willie said.

"Enchanting," Nick replied.

The door was slightly ajar. Nick wondered if they should ring the bell or just walk in. Perhaps the door had been left open so they didn't have to ring. He rang anyway. When no-one answered, he knocked. Again, no-one answered. Slowly, he pushed the door open. Willie followed, camera rolling and perched on his shoulder.

The house stank. It smelled of mold and stale air and rotten food. They entered the kitchen cautiously, measuring their steps, like detectives at a crime scene. A macabre scene greeted them. All of the lights were off. The only light came from candles, which had been placed at various points on the floor and on the table. Black candles. Short, stubby black candles. And hanging from a chain just above the table was a large, inverted cross with a figure of Jesus attached. What appeared to be real blood dripped from the figure onto the white ceramic table top. Dishes and silverware, caked with food, were piled high in the sink, spilling out onto the counters, which were layered with grease and grime. Roaches crawled around in the mess. Nick and Willie exchanged a worried look before moving, cautiously, into the living room.

There a much worse scene awaited them. A middle-aged man with a bulging belly lay on a chair, head back, face contorted in pain, with blood dripping down his chin, and his fat, blubbery arms dangling limply at his sides. His fat, hairy stomach had been torn open—presumably with a knife—and his legs stretched out in front of him in a wide V. He wore nothing but a pair of shorts and a tank top T-shirt. And written in blood on the wall were the words:

"I form the light, and create darkness: I make peace and CREATE EVIL…." (Isa. 45:7)

"Jesus Christ," Nick gasped.

"This is some bad shit," Willie added, even as he panned in on the horrific scene with his camera. The two men had seen some strange things in the line of duty, but nothing like this. Not even close. Now Nick knew where that feeling of dread came from. This place was bad. But even worse than the carnage was what he felt. The feeling…. The *Spirit* that was in the air in this place.

The prince of the power of the air, who is at work in the sons of disobedience….

Infesting the air like a thick, palpable mist was a feeling of utter and absolute hatred—a hatred that ran deeper than a thousand oceans and burned hotter than a thousand suns. Raw, naked hatred. And the rage that attended it. This was a place where there was *no* light, and, for a moment, Nick had the strange and terrifying sensation that God Himself was not there.

"What do you want to do?" Willie asked. "Call the cops?"

"No," Nick said. There were still three more people in the home and they had to see what happened to them. And besides, something told Nick that the cops would be of no use to them.

"Come on, let's check the bedrooms," Nick said. He led the way as Willie followed with his camera.

The bedrooms offered more gruesome discoveries. In one they found an elderly woman in a nightgown lying in bed with a large railroad stake protruding from the space between her eyes; in the other a child hanging upside down and naked from the ceiling, gutted down middle, with his intestines hanging out.

That was enough for Nick. "Come on," he said to Willie, "Let's get out of here. We can call the cops from the car."

Neither man had to say the obvious, namely, that the old man — the "possessed party" — was responsible for the slayings. And neither particularly wished to confront him at this time. Unfortunately for them, that had ceased to be an option.

As they re-entered the living room, the old man was there, waiting for them. He was sitting in a chair, opposite the wall with the bloody bible verse, facing them. He wore a pair of boxer shorts and a sleeveless T-shirt. He had white hair, a thin, straggly goatee, and a gaunt, pale face. Gently, he rocked back and forth in the chair, looking right at them with wide, dead eyes. Those eyes were grey and lifeless, and Nick knew that the person they belonged to had long since left the building. Whatever looked through those eyes now, he sensed, was not a person at all, but something dark and sinister, and seething with an inconceivable, ancient malevolence — a malevolence far deeper than any human could muster, one born of a trauma suffered eons ago in another realm. It was the hatred of demons cast out of heaven and committed to chains of darkness, where they awaited a certain and awful doom.

The man held a shotgun, with the barrel pointed toward the ceiling. He held it loosely, caressing the barrel with his hand, as if shining it. He smiled and said, "Thanks for coming, Nick. I knew you wouldn't let me down."

When Nick said nothing in response, Willie said, "It's okay. We're here to help."

The old man's smile grew wider. "Well, thank you," he said. "That's mighty kind of you. But I don't need no help. And besides, this is gonna be great for your ratings. You're gonna be a star, Nick."

Then he pressed the barrel of the gun up against the bottom of his chin and blew off the top of his head.

Chapter 2

Cassie Gallo hung up the phone and turned on the nightly news. She had just gotten off the phone with Nick, who had filled her in on all of the details: the house, the slayings, the old man, the police, etc.... The aftermath of a horrific murder, and a suicide, captured live, on film. And it would all be on the news tonight. That's what he told her, and he was right. There it was, up on the screen — Nick, standing in front of a cordoned off crime scene, talking to a reporter from the Channel 5 news.

He had wanted her to hear it from him before she heard it on TV, and for that she was grateful. He had told her all about it, and said he was on his way home. For that she was even more grateful.

The report featured some of the footage Willie had captured, although with most of the gore edited out. After all, it was a news show, not a snuff film. Just the same, it was horrifying. She watched, transfixed, at the incredible carnage, and could scarcely imagine Nick's reaction upon stumbling into such a scene. When it was over, she shut the TV off and just sat there, staring at the blank screen, thinking about Nick and their lives together.

She had met Nick at a church social twenty-five years

ago. It wasn't quite love at first sight, but there was definitely a connection. They each had their separate careers at that point—she a nurse and he a tax auditor—and neither planned a life in the ministry. But they both loved the Lord, and as their love for Him—and for each other—grew, their calling became clear. Nick enrolled in a local Bible college, still working part-time as an accountant, while she continued her nursing. Upon graduation, he secured a position as an Associate Pastor with The Sword of the Spirit Pentecostal Church in Pine Hill Park, New Jersey.

And that's when his star began to rise. At Sword of the Spirit, Nick was in his element. Born and raised in the Charismatic movement, he was at home with all things supernatural. Dreams. Visions. Miraculous healings. Speaking in tongues. And yes, even exorcisms. His was a faith of experience, of ecstasy. A faith of sight and sound and feel and touch and taste. And so when he took the helm of a Pentecostal church, a dramatic surge in the character of the services was sure to follow. And it did. The services quickly morphed from dry rituals of songs and sermons into sweat-soaked orgies of spiritual ecstasy. Not surprisingly, donations swelled. Soon word spread and the church had more worshippers than it could contain in an average sized building on a modestly sized corner property. So they purchased the vacant lot next door, joined the buildings together, and just like that, a mega-church was born. But more than just a church. A ministry. A movement. A mission. Advertising on local TV followed. Then billboards. Internet. Radio adds. And so on. The church became a phenomenon.

Next thing they knew, Hollywood came calling. They sent a talent scout to check out one of their services. He loved what he saw and offered Nick his own cable show. Basically, it was nothing more than a televised Sunday service, but, given the nature of the service, it made for some pretty good television. Nick even locked horns with the devil, casting demons out of the tortured souls who filled the church every week. Sometimes they came from hundreds of miles away to experience his healing touch. That portion of the show proved so popular that it spawned a spin-off—*Into the Devil's Den*—a program which saw Nick taking his show on the road, traveling across the tri-state area in search of demonic activity.

Along with making them a lot of money, the shows had made her and Nick local celebrities. She did not mind the attention. Most people were nice. The critics, of course, were a different story. Most of them dismissed the show as a contrived display of religious theatrics and chicanery. Most, but not all. And most of those in the evangelical community accepted her and Nick as sincere members of the faith.

As for Nick, he was sincere. Up to a point. He did believe in God, in the devil, in the inerrancy of scripture, in the power of prayer, and in the prophetic word. And when he first started out, he believed in demon possession, too. Several hundred "exorcisms" later, however, he realized that he was not battling Satan so much as mental illness. But that was okay. He believed there was a fine line between mental illness and Satanic activity. After all, wasn't all evil, in the final analysis, traceable to Satan? Did not even Christ ascribe a physical ailment, in the case of the crippled woman, to Satan? Besides, the exorcisms really did seem to help, so where was the harm?

As for her part, she no longer believed in any of it. Not

a word. To her it had all come to seem so absurd: a canon of Scripture compiled over the course of hundreds of years, littered with known forgeries, shaped by imperial politics and the sword, differing from one sect to another, and from one epoch to another, whose proper translation is a matter of debate, and whose meaning no two scholars agree upon, all centered around a Savior who expressly promised to return during the lifetime of the apostles, and didn't, and which offers no consistent answer for the single most pressing problem all people face — the problem of suffering.

And yet, we are to believe, if we don't place our faith in this canon, whose meaning, translation, and authorship, is anyone's guess, and in this Savior, who promised to return 2,000 years ago and didn't, we will be punished forever in hell.

Well, she could no longer buy it. Unfortunately, she was still in the business of selling it. And she didn't have the courage to stop. This was her job. Her station in life. It was who everyone thought she was. It was who everyone expected her to be. It was who she had spent years learning how to be. It was all she knew. It was her identity. How could she possibly just up and tell the world — or even Nick — that suddenly this person, Cassie Gallo, partner in Sword of the Spirit Ministries and faithful servant of the Lord, was an utter, abject, absolute lie? That almost everything she said to almost everyone she met, both personally and professionally, was a big, fat, steaming pile of horseshit? That every compliment she received, every award she accepted, every check she cashed, was done so under false pretenses? How could she do that?

She couldn't. She did not have the courage.

And so she would continue to keep up the charade. She would continue promising to pray for people for when she knew prayer would not help. She would continue to assure the bereaved that their loved ones were in heaven when she had not a clue where they really were. She would even continue to offer the same rote, brain-dead explanations to people looking for answers to life's riddles. Why do babies die? Original sin. Where do they go? Heaven, of course, as they have not yet reached the "age of accountability." Why does suffering exist? Free will. What about Gandhi; is he in hell? Probably not, but who knows?

And so on. They were the answers one found in the troubleshooting section of the manual that governed her particular brand of religious faith. Yes, it was bullshit. She knew that. And she had simply come to accept that she was in the bullshit business. Like a salesperson. She was just selling her product; that's what she told herself. Was it really any worse than selling used cars?

In some ways, it was better. She never had to look someone in the eye and tell an outright lie, such as "This carburetor works fine" when she knew it didn't. She couldn't *know* God would not answer the prayers she offered; she couldn't *know* a baby wasn't dead because of original sin; she couldn't *know* a mother's child wasn't in heaven. She was just making guesses; telling people what they wanted to hear in the absence of any real answers. Isn't that what everyone does to some degree? How else do you get through the day? At least that's what she told herself, and had been telling herself for a long time now. But with each passing day it became harder to believe.

She envied Nick. He knew his place in the world. Just like she used to. And when doubts came — and he did have them—he was able to squash them with the usual answers. Not completely, but enough to keep them from upsetting his theological applecart. Sometimes she felt like looking him dead in the eyes and shouting: "How can you keep believing all this bullshit? Don't you have a fucking brain?!"

But she didn't. Instead, she simply pretended to believe it too. After all, their shared beliefs were an integral part of their marriage. It was a big part—the biggest part—of why they got married. They shared the same worldview, the same faith, the same moral code. To suddenly tell him that she no longer shared that code would be almost like telling him that she was really a man. What would happen? She didn't know.

And therein lay the terror of it. She had spent her whole life taking the safe route. Doing what was expected. Avoiding the unknown. Embracing the Christian way of life was really just a way of making her cowardice into a virtue. She could walk the straight and narrow, avoiding all of life's risks and perils, not out of fear, but out of principle. And she was not prepared, at forty-eight years of age, to suddenly veer off into unknown territory.

No, she had made her deal with the devil and she would keep it. Some had it worse. A lot worse. So, she didn't have the courage of her convictions. She did not live true to her ideals. Okay. She could live with that. Not happily, perhaps.

But at least securely.

Chapter 3

Pastor Terrence Baker could feel the car coming to a stop as he lay there, bound and gagged, in the trunk. He did not know where he was. He did not know what his abductors wanted with him. And he did not know if he would make it out of this alive. But he did know one thing: the last few months had seen a rash of murders in the tri-state area. Four in all. All of them members of the clergy, either Catholic or Protestant. All killed in the worst way conceivable. And by the looks of things, he might well be on his way to becoming victim number five.

He heard car doors slam closed and two sets of feet moving about. His captors had arrived at their destination. Soon he would find out what they wanted with him. And what they had wanted with the others—assuming the ones who abducted him were the same ones that abducted the others. The ones who had declared WAR ON RELIGION, publishing their depraved manifesto in a local newspaper.

He heard a sound, like metal doors being flung open. Next thing he knew the trunk popped open and he found himself staring at his abductors—a man and a woman.

The woman he recognized, but not the man. The man grabbed him by the torso, the woman by the legs, and together they hoisted him out of the trunk. Next they dragged him down a small flight of cement steps and down into a cellar. There they dumped him while the man ran back up the steps to close the cellar doors. He came back down and stood by the woman.

Helplessly, Terrence looked up at them as they hovered above him, staring down. Their faces were masks of thinly disguised contempt. These people did not like him. That he knew instantly. It was personal with them. Something about him made something in them angry as hell. He suspected it had more than a little to do with the fact that he was the pastor of a church.

He watched as the man walked over to a door and opened it. Then the man came back for him, grabbed him under his arm-pits and dragged him toward the door, and into the room behind it. The woman followed.

He looked around. The room consisted of wooden cedar planks, which lined the walls and the floors. Along the walls were benches. It was a sauna. Mounted in a corner was a wall unit television with a DVD player on a shelf beneath it.

The man dragged Terrence over to the corner, by one of the benches, right next to a steel pipe that ran from the floor to the ceiling. The pipe had a chain with a shackle attached. The man took a switchblade out of his pocket, cut the ropes on Terry's hands, then slipped his right hand into the shackle. He worked matter-of-factly, saying nothing. The feet he simply left tied. Lastly, he took the gag out of Terry's mouth. Terry knew better than to scream, and he could tell his abductors knew that.

He looked at his captors. The woman he knew. She

was of medium height and build, and had long wavy black hair and big brown eyes. She was gorgeous. The man looked kind of like a fifties biker, with slicked back hair, a white tee shirt beneath a black jacket, and matching black pants and boots.

They were both middle-aged—in their forties, he guessed. For several moments he just sat there, chained to the pipe, saying nothing, as they stared right back at him. Each party was accessing the other, with neither one speaking. About a minute passed, then the woman sauntered up to him, tickled the bottom of his chin with one hand, and said "Sorry it had to end this way, dearie." Then, slowly, she bent down, placed her lips inches from his ear, and whispered "But you know what they say about the wages of sin." Then she breathed gently into his ear, and licked his earlobe. He shuddered in spite of himself at the woman's touch. She straightened back up and looked down at him with a bemused smile on her face. The smile said: *You poor dear, I'm going to enjoy killing you.*

He was almost as embarrassed as he was afraid, if that was possible. How had he allowed this to happen? How did he allow himself to be seduced by this woman? And now this. Was this his punishment? After 20 years of faithful service in the ministry, was he to go out like this? In a blaze of infamy and disgrace? Dying for Christ was one thing. That he could accept, and perhaps face with courage. But to die because he stepped into a harlot's lure—that he could not bear. He couldn't go out like this. He had to escape.

The man finally broke the silence, saying simply: "I guess you're wondering why you're here." He spoke with a thinly veiled layer of contempt, like a dyspeptic DMV worker.

"Yes, I am," Terrence said. Without saying a word, the man walked over to the DVD player, picked up the remote control, and turned on the television. The opening credits rolled. They read: A production of the First Baptist Church of Sycamore, New Jersey. That was Terrence's church. The video was titled *Halloween in Hell*.

Terrence and a few members of the church had made the video about a decade ago. The concept was simple: Basically, it was the Christian equivalent of Scared Straight, with kids treated to a vignette of ghastly visions depicting the torment that awaited those who committed certain sins. A woman splattered in blood lay on a gurney as doctors stabbed her repeatedly with the very same objects employed to perform her abortion. A gay man is strapped to a bed while men clad in black leather flog him mercilessly. A whore is roasted alive over burning hot coals. Similar scenes play out for similar sins. But the theme is always the same; your sins catch up to you. And without Jesus as your Savior, you die in them, and suffer never-ending torment.

The man waited for the final credits, then shut off the TV. Then he sat down beside Terrence and looked straight at him, his face a mask of contempt. A moment passed, then, suddenly, he spit in Terrence's face. As the spit rolled slowly down his face, the woman sauntered up behind the man, and put a hand on his shoulder. "Come on, be nice," she said. It was not a tone that betrayed any compassion, just a desire to keep things neat and clean and to get on with business.

The man smiled at her, then looked back at Terrence. He had taken her advice; the anger was gone from his face. He extended his hand to Terrence, and the two men shook hands.

"My name is Austin," the man said in a cordial voice. "And this is Samantha...as you already know."

He said the last words without sarcasm, merely as a statement of fact. His tone gave Terrence a faint hope that he might be dealing with someone who could be reasoned with, at least on some level. A maniac, perhaps; a killer, undoubtedly; but still someone who might be open to intelligent discourse; after all, even crazy people did not act without motive. *Everyone* had their reasons; maybe if he could understand the ones that motivated this man, then maybe, just maybe, there was a chance. A hope. He had to have at least that.

"My name is Terrence Baker," the pastor said, knowing full well that they already knew who he was. But did he know who they were? Were they the ones who he had been reading about? He didn't ask; at this point, he didn't *want* to know. It might cloud his judgment, his ability to remain calm and to reason with these folks. And if he needed anything right now, it was to stay calm. Already his suit was sopped in sweat; his heart pounded in his chest, and his head felt fuzzy and light. It would not take much from where he now stood to push him over the edge. There was a fine line between high anxiety — even terror — and full-blown panic, and he could not afford to cross it at this time. If he was to have any chance — *any* chance — of getting out of there alive, he had to keep his cool.

"We know who you are," Austin said. As he spoke, Samantha took a seat on the bench on the opposite wall. "Let me tell you why you're here, chief," Austin said.

Ah, yes, the man thought, *the sixty four thousand dollar question. I knew there had to be some reason I was here. Please, tell me what it is.*

"You are here because this, chief, is the way it has to be. You see, I'm not a violent man."

That was something Terrence was glad to hear, but had a lot of trouble believing.

"I never wanted to hurt anyone," Austin continued. "I wish it didn't have to come to this. I wish that folks like you and me could just agree to disagree. But here's the thing; you won't do that."

Austin rubbed his hands across his face and through his hair, like people do when trying to communicate a particularly elusive thought. "Do you know what I mean when I say 'you won't agree to disagree'?"

Before Terrence could answer, Austin answered his own question. "I mean, you don't respect people's right to disagree. You do everything you can to convince people that if they don't think like you, act like you, pray like you, believe like you, they are going straight to hell. Oh, sure, you can say: We don't put a gun to no-one's head. But don't you, pastor? What about the kids on that tape? Were they free to disagree? To just turn and walk away? And what about the ones even younger than that? They can't walk away. They're born into a prison that folks like you created and they have to live in it every minute until they're old enough to run, and by then they're minds are too warped to even want to run. By then they believe the lies they were raised on and feed those lies to their young, and the cycle just goes on and on and on, forever, with no end in sight. Institutionalized brainwashing.

"You see, chief; there's only one way to deal with folks like you. Only one language you understand. Force. All around the world people are abusing each other in the name of religion. In the name of God, they scare, bully, coerce, enslave, mutilate, and even kill each other. And nobody is standing up to them. Nobody is returning fire. Well, no more, chief. I'm taking a stand. I'm drawing a line in the sand. I'm saying: Enough!"

Terrence's hopes sank as Austin's voice rose and the calm words of reason gave way to the rantings of an avenging crusader. Not a good sign.

"I am declaring war on Preachers," Austin continued, "War on Pastors, War on Priests, War on Church, War on Altar Boys, War on Choir Boys, War on Catholics, War on Protestants, War on Methodists, War on Baptists, War on Pentecostals, War on Episcopalians, War on Lutherans, War on Presbyterians, War on Anglicans, War on Eastern Orthodox, War on Mormons, War on Jehovah's Witnesses, War on Sunnis, War on Shias, War on Religion, War on God!"

Terrence began to realize what he was dealing with. Here was a man with a full blown messiah complex, no different than that of a David Koresh or a Charles Manson; only with the added twist of God as enemy rather than friend.

Terrence could take it no longer; he had to know for sure. And so he asked: "Are you the ones who published the letter? The ones who committed those murders?"

"Oh, yes, that was us," Austin answered.

Terrence felt like a fifty pound anchor had just dropped in his stomach. He did not want to die, but for God's sake, he didn't want to die like the other victims. They had been roasted to death.

Stephen Campana

Chapter 4

As Dr. Adam Becker stared at his patient, Martin Monroe, lying helplessly in bed, his once able body now emaciated and weak, his once sound mind now torn and tortured, he could not help but feel grateful that he was an atheist. This is what religion did to people. Catholic guilt, an old girlfriend used to call it. She was a Catholic, not him. He was a non-practicing, nonbelieving Jew, and proud of it. It's not that he hated religion, or religious people; he just did not see any point to it. He knew of no good and lofty command, precept, ideal, or law, derived from religion that was not also prized by the non-religious. It was only the bad things that needed justification by Revelation. We could all love without God. We could not all pilot planes into towers without Him. We could all care for our children without God. We could not sacrifice them on altars without Him. We could all be sorry for our sins without God. We could not all mutilate ourselves for them without Him. Then what good is He? What does He add to the collective consciousness of humanity that we would not have without Him? Nothing, as far as Adam could tell.

And without Him, we would not have cases like Martin Monroe. If ever there was a victim of Catholic guilt, it was him. Abused by a priest at a young age, he grew up consumed with guilt, blaming himself for the crime, and receiving more blame by his parents, who, not surprisingly, dismissed his story. What, a priest do something like *that*! Shame on you. Get in the closet for a few hours; that will teach you to smear the holy clergy, you impertinent little prick.

Not surprisingly, he grew up to hate priests. And religion. And himself. Himself most of all. He talked to no-one about his shame; he just repressed it, pushing it as far down as it would go, until his conscious mind hardly even remembered it anymore. But it was still there, of course, seething like a poison, and poisoning everything he touched—all of his friendships, all of his relationships, all attempts at a normal life. He could not function normal sexually, and became confused about that part of his life. Adam had detected tendencies toward homosexuality and pedophilia. It was all too much for him. All he could do was push it down, blaming himself. He began to think he was evil. Not just everyday evil, but really super extraordinary evil. As in possessed by a demon. Gradually he took on more and more of the classic symptoms of a "possessed" person, until he had essentially morphed into an adult male equivalent of Linda Blair's character in *The Exorcist*, complete with throaty voice, facial sores, rotten teeth, and other assorted grotesque manifestations. And Like Blair's character, he switched back and forth between himself and his alter ego, or "demon."

It was really quite a show. And now, one with a new twist: Martin was demanding an exorcism. It was not hard for Adam to understand why. It was easier. It was easier to regard your evil as an occupying force that could be expelled in one fell swoop by an ancient ritual rather than something in-built that had to be treated with intensive therapy. This, combined with the fact that Martin believed himself to be evil, led to his delusion that he was possessed.

Normally, Adam would have dismissed the idea of an exorcism out of hand. But he had ample reason to believe it might not be such a bad idea. If a person truly believed themselves possessed, then an exorcism could provide them with a certain measure of relief. It was the placebo effect: A person who believes they are taking a pill that will cure them is likely to feel better, even if the pill is nothing more than a sugar cube. Moreover, Martin had reached a point where he was beyond the help of conventional therapy. As long as he believed the problem was evil, he would remain immune to any and all therapeutic techniques. And Adam had tried them all. Now, he had come to believe, it was time to try something new. It was time to give him his exorcism.

Normally, this would pose a problem. Exorcisms were the province of Catholic priests. And the Catholic Church did not just hand out exorcisms like it handed out those wafers you got at the end of mass. No, it was a process. They had to qualify you. Fortunately, he would not have to worry about any of that. That's because Martin did not want a Catholic priest to exorcise him. In fact, he had requested by name the man he wished to perform the rite. A Protestant Pastor and televangelist by the name of Nick Gallo.

Adam had heard of Gallo. He did not know much about him, but from what he gathered, the man was your typical charlatan, pitching his snake oil on TV to poor, deluded souls willing who wanted to believe he could cure them of their ills, be they physical or spiritual.

No matter. This was not about what really worked — only about what Martin *thought* would work. And if he thought Nick Gallo could help him, then maybe, just maybe, he could.

Chapter 5

Cassie Gallo stared somberly at the inscription on the gravestone. It read: Raymond Gallo—1990–2009. Age eighteen. That's when her son killed himself. Swallowed too many pills. They called it an accidental overdose. But she knew it wasn't.

She knelt down, one knee in the dirt, pressed an open palm against the tombstone, then slid her hand across its surface in slow, gentle circles, as if caressing it. This was the closest she would ever get to touching her son again.

Cassie went to the cemetery about once a month. She went alone. Nick did not even know about it. She didn't tell him. There was no need, no point. The truth was she went there to be alone with her son. And she did not want their communion tainted by the presence by anyone who did not love and accept him for exactly who—and what—he was. And that included Nick.

Raymond was gay. He was born gay. Practically from birth, he was not like other boys. He preferred dolls to trucks; he'd rather play house than cowboys and Indians; and he gravitated to the girls rather than the boys in school. It seemed harmless enough at first, even cute. But after a few years, it became a cause for concern. And so she and Nick responded the way lots of parents respond in those situations: they tried to change their son. They tried to steer him toward the "right" toys, the right games, the right activities, and the right kids. And when it wasn't working.... Well, they just kept trying. Through childhood into the tween years and right into young adulthood. Their goal was always the same: get Raymond on the right path. Set him straight. Correct him. And when the preference of dolls over sports evolved into a preference of boys over girls, well, that's when *real* correction was necessary. They brought him to counselors. Psychiatrists. Ministers. They brought him to Christian counselors who specialized in "curing" his sinful predilection, and restoring him to "health." And of course, they never, ever told any friends, neighbors, or family. Oh, they loved their son, and he knew it. But he was fundamentally—and fatally—flawed, and he knew that too. And it wasn't an ordinary, everyday flaw, like a club foot or stuttering; it was a *major* flaw—a moral defect—and it could cause him to be damned forever in the Lake of Fire, which Scripture said was reserved for "fornicators, idolaters, adulterers, and *effeminate*...."

Like any good parent, they did not want their son to go to hell; hence they made it their life's work to cure him of the sin that was leading him down that path. But as the years went by and their efforts all went for naught, she began to have her doubts. Maybe this wasn't something they could correct. Maybe they had to either accept their son, lock, stock, and barrel, for who and what he was—or not—with no middle ground. Either love him or hate him. Embrace him, or try to fix him. Slowly, she began to do the former.

Nick did not. And Raymond knew it. He knew she

loved him unconditionally, with a mother's love, and that Nick did not. Oh, she still kept up appearances. She never directly challenged Nick's efforts to change their son, but gradually she ceased to be an active partner in those efforts. She merely went along. It was lip service. And so she and Raymond had come to share a different kind of relationship than the one he had with his father.

And that's why she came to the cemetery alone. She loved her son in a way Nick never could. She didn't *care* if God didn't love Him; *she* loved him. Fuck God. She loved him more than she loved God. And if God couldn't love him the way *He* created him—yes, it was not a *choice*—then fuck God, too. God does not need our help, our flattery, our applause, and our approval. People do. That's what she had come to believe, what she still believed, and what she would believe for the rest of her life. If God loved Raymond, then he was in His arms right now in Heaven. Without any question. And if He didn't love the *gay* Raymond, then He had never loved Raymond to begin with. That much she knew for certain. If Raymond, or any other soul who ever lived, was damned, it was because it was God's intention from the start to damn them, and not because the soul had turned out other than expected, or had overthrown God's plans for them, to His great grief.

After Raymond's death, she came to a point, secretly, where she hated her religion. And herself, for still being a part of it. And maybe Nick, too—and the Church, and the Catholics, and the Protestants, and the Pastors, and the Priests, and the Church Ladies, and the Church Men, and the hypocritical Church Laity, and the Altar Boys, and the Pope, and the World, and God Himself. It was a hatred she had buried deep inside herself, and one that she could control, but it was real just the same. She knew just how real when recently, as she read about the gruesome murders of pastors in the tri-state area, she found herself feeling a twinge of satisfaction.

Cassie straightened herself up and wiped the soil off her knees with her hands. Then she gently kissed her hand, placed it on the top of the tombstone, and moved it slowly back and forth over the rough surface of the stone. Then she bowed her head, turned around, and slowly walked back to her car.

She would see him again next month.

Chapter 6

Donald Dennett, the River View Hospital Administrator, looked across his desk at Adam Becker, trying to think of how to respond to the idea the young man had just suggested.

He liked Adam. He was one of the youngest and brightest members of the staff at Toluca Hill's *River View Mental Facility.* Only thirty years of age, he had already distinguished himself as a therapist of exceptional skill, uncommon compassion, and wisdom beyond his years. And more importantly than any of that, he trusted Adam's judgment. In the young man's brief, but impressive, tenure at *River View* his recommendations always seemed to be on the mark.

Except maybe this time. Donald liked to think of himself as open-minded and progressive. He was not averse to new ideas. But this one gave him pause. Major pause. An *exorcism*? That posed three problems. First, *River View* was a state run facility. They were obliged to maintain a separation of church and state. Secondly, this kind of a "treatment" was fraught with peril. Essentially, it would reinforce the very delusion that they, as mental health professionals, were trying to dispel. Moreover, it might make things worse. And third, why would the Catholic Church even sanction such a thing? Did they not demand concrete evidence of actual possession? Evidence which, in this case, did not exist?

"I don't know about this, Adam," Donald said. "It sounds a little bit...." He searched for the right word, trying his best to be diplomatic.

"Crazy?" Adam suggested.

"Well.... Yes," Donald said. "I was going to say *unorthodox*, but I think crazy fits the bill even better."

Adam smiled. "I know how it sounds," he said, "but hear me out."

"Gladly," Donald said.

"This guy has been at *River View* for two years now. We've tried everything on him. Every kind of drug, every kind of therapy. Nothing has worked. He's just kept getting worse."

"I can't argue with that," Donald said.

"So when nothing is working, what do we do? We try something new, right?"

"Yes, we try a new *therapy*," Donald replied.

"Come on, Mr. Dennett," Adam said, "You've seen this guy. Do you really think *any* conventional therapy is going to work on him?"

Donald said nothing. His silence said all there was to say.

Adam pressed his advantage. "So isn't that a good reason to consider something new? Maybe even something...unorthodox?"

"Well...yes, but an *exorcism*? We are a state run facility. We have to maintain a separation of church and state."

"I know, I know," Adam said, anticipating the objection. "But patients get visits from their pastors, right? They're allowed to have bibles, to pray. Sometimes the staff even prays with them."

"But that's a far cry from a formal religious ritual."

"But that's the thing. This wouldn't really be a formal ritual exorcism."

"How so?"

"Well, formal exorcisms are performed by Catholic priests. They require the sanction of the Catholic Church. But this guy isn't asking for a priest; he's asking for a pastor. And he even has one in mind — Nick Gallo."

"Nick Gallo," Donald repeated. "I've heard of him. He's that.... That demon hunter guy, isn't he?"

"Yep."

"Okay, so let's say we did bring this guy in. What's the difference between what he would do and what a priest would do?"

"Well, first off, you don't need to get any kind of official church approval. And secondly, Protestants don't perform exorcisms the same way as Catholics. It's less ritual, more prayer. Kind of an extended prayer of deliverance."

Donald sighed. "I don't know, Adam. This Nick Gallo guy; from what I gather he likes to perform his *prayers* for an audience."

"Well, needless to say; this one would not be filmed."

Donald shook his head, a look of resignation creeping onto his face. "I'll tell you what," he said, "You try and contact this Gallo guy. Feel him out on it. If he's willing to see Martin, we can arrange for a meeting. No exorcism, no prayers of deliverance; not yet. Just a meeting. An assessment. Let the two men talk for a while and then we can take it from there."

Adam extended a hand across the desk. "It's a deal," he said. Donald shook Adam's hand and smiled at the young man. He reminded him of himself—thirty years ago. Only Adam was smarter and better looking.

"I hope I'm not going to regret this," Donald said.

"Me too," Adam replied, smiling.

Chapter 7

For the thousandth time that day, Terrence Baker tugged on the chain that kept him bound to the pipe that ran down the length of the sauna room. The result was the same as the first nine hundred and ninety nine times. Nothing. The chain didn't give; the shackle on his wrist didn't give; and the pipe didn't give. Not even a little. If he wanted to escape, he had better devise a better plan than tugging on the thick iron chain that bound him by a thick iron shackle to a thick iron pipe.

He looked around. He was surrounded by wood. Wooden cedar planks. On the floor, on the ceiling, on the walls. And wooden benches running along the sides of the room, parallel to the walls. He felt like a toy soldier trapped in a tiny matchstick prison. He was, in a sense. He was their toy, their plaything, their pawn in their little war on God.

In the corner was a heater with pipes running from it into the walls, and valves attached to the pipes at various points. Up on the wall was a thermometer with two readings—one that measured temperature and another that measured humidity. He knew that much from the steams he took at the YMCA.

He had been there for three days now. Three days sitting—sometimes lying down—on a bench on one side of a wooden box, staring at the heater in the corner of the other side of the room. The chain affixed to his arm was not long enough to allow him access to the door or the heater. It was long enough, however, to allow him access to a bucket, which he used to relieve himself, and a water bottle. Those were his only two amenities. Several times a day the woman came in to dump the bucket. During that ritual, she held a gun on him to make sure he didn't try anything.

Terrence hung his head between his knees, looking down at the wooden cedar planks beneath his feet. He had to figure out a way to escape. He could not go out like this. Not as a sinner. Not as an adulterer.

His mind drifted back to the events that led to his capture.

He first saw the woman—Samantha—about a year ago. He was sitting in the altar area waiting to give his Sunday sermon when he noticed her. She was impossible not to notice. She was sitting in the front row, wearing a thin, summery dress that showed a lot of chest and leg. Normally, the dress would have seemed inappropriate, but given that it was a scorching mid-July day, it seemed okay. At any rate, she sat there, legs crossed, staring at him with smoldering eyes as he sat waiting to give his sermon. Every so often her hand would slide slowly down her leg, to her high heel pumps, and then back up again. A gleam seemed to creep into her eyes when she did this. And she did it repeatedly throughout the entire service.

He tried not to look, but he found his eyes irresistibly drawn to her. Even as he gave his sermon, he could not help himself from sneaking peaks. Each time he did, he hoped she didn't notice. And for the most part, she gave no sign that she did. Then, toward the end of the service, her eyes caught his—caught him looking—and a small, wry smile crept across her lips, a smile that said: "I see you looking, you naughty boy." He felt humiliated, like a child caught peeping at his sister or something. He didn't know why he felt so embarrassed; he just did. Maybe it was because he was so incredibly attracted to this woman. Maybe it was because she seemed to know it, and seemed to *like* it.

A few days later, at night, he received a phone call while working in his office. It was her. She said she needed to speak with him. He arranged a meeting for the next day. She showed up wearing the same dress. He invited her to sit down on the chair next to his desk. She obliged, crossing her legs the same way she had in church. She smelled wonderful.

At first, the conversation seemed harmless enough. She shared some details about her past, recounted a few experiences, told a few anecdotes. Nothing too heavy. But when she got down to discussing her "problem"...well, things got heated. That's when she leaned forward, her face close to his, and said in a whisper: *I think the devil's gotten control of my....* She paused and looked down at her lap. *Of my...private parts.* After saying those words, she stared at him, wide-eyed, her face a mask of horrified anticipation. She had looked to him, in that moment, like a little child revealing what she believed to be a terrible, magical secret. Sweating, Terrence said, "Tell me why you think that."

She sighed and folded her hands across her stomach, as if she had a tummy ache. "It makes things happen down there," she said, looking down at her crotch, embarrassed.

"What kind of things?" Terrence asked, knowing that he was crossing a dangerous line.

"Bad things," the woman said, her voice crackling with a kind of awkward arousal.

"Are you feeling them right now?" Terrence had asked.

"Yeah," the woman groaned, her breath becoming labored. "I'm feeling it…right…now." She clenched her thighs together, as if trying to smother a fire beneath her legs.

"It's okay," Terrence said. "You don't have to fight it."

Her fidgeting intensified. "It's just so…embarrassing." She sighed, her face contorting with a mixture of pain and pleasure. Then she uncrossed her legs, turned her knees and feet inward, and pressed both of her hands down hard between her legs, as if trying to hold in a pee. "Oh, God," she had groaned, looking at him helplessly, almost pleadingly. "I…can't…stop it," she gasped.

"It's okay," he said, watching as the beautiful woman in his church office was swept up in a massive orgasm.

When it was finished, she let out a huge sigh and leaned back in her chair, breathing heavily. The smell of her sex seeped through her panties, mingling with her perfume, and it gave him a massive erection. She buried her face in her hands. "Oh, God," she cried, "I'm so sorry, I'm so sorry."

"It's okay," he assured her, feeling like a leech and a liar.

"I'm so sorry," she said again, then reached across the desk and placed a hand on his. "I'm sorry, did I…arouse you?" She sounded like a mother asking her child if she had hurt him.

Caught off guard, Nick stammered for an answer.

"No, no," the woman said, patting his hand. "It's okay; it was my fault. I'm sorry. I'm so sorry."

Nick was at a complete loss for words.

"Look," she said. "This isn't the place to deal with this problem. Here's what I'm going to do." She took a post-it from his desk and began writing. "I'm going to give you my name and number, and if you ever feel that you can help me, please, please call me." Then she handed him the post-it. He took it without saying a word. Then she stood up, ironed out her skirt with her hands, and leaned forward, inches from his face. The smell of her sweat and perfume made Nick swoon. "Thank you," she whispered, her voice tickling the inside of his ear in a way that made his whole body tingle. Then she kissed him on the cheek and left.

He did not see her again for a year. But he had kept the name and number. And sometimes, when he was in the shower, or on the toilet, or alone in bed, he thought about her and jerked off to the traces of her voice, her smell, her face, that had remained in his memory. And during those times, he sometimes found himself thinking: *What if I called her? What's the harm? She asked for my help? Don't I have an obligation to help her?*

During this time his marriage was drifting. And each time it hit a rock, he found himself thinking about making that call. Thinking about it and then resisting. Then one day, after a titanic argument, his wife stormed off to spend a few days with her sister. Alone, angry, and depressed, Terrence could no longer resist. He called the number she had written on the post-it. Even as he called, even as he met her at the motel she recommended, he had not admitted to himself — or her — the real reason. He was still clinging to the fantasy that he was trying to help her, or maybe, just maybe, he just needed someone to talk to at that moment, and maybe she could help him; maybe they could help each other.

They met at the motel. They had a drink. Next thing he knew, he felt sick. Too sick to drive. She volunteered to drive him to the hospital. He got into her car, and the next thing he knew, a hand reached around from the backseat and pressed an ammonia-soaked towel against his face. Moments later, he lost consciousness. When he awoke, he was bound and gagged in the trunk of the car.

That was about three days ago. Three days of being chained to a pipe in a basement sauna. The man had left. Where he went, Terrence didn't know. But he gathered that he did not live there. It was the woman's residence. A few times a day, she came to check on him, to feed him, to change the bucket. It was all very deliberate, very calculated, and very matter-of-fact. No talking. He gathered that she shared the man's contempt for him, but not quite to the same extent. Something told him this was more his crusade than hers. She was a soldier; he was the general. And that gave him hope. Maybe there was some way to reach her. That was one possibility.

The other was escape. How he might do that, he hadn't a clue, but there had to be a way. He had to get out, and it had to be soon. Before the man returned, before the torture started. The other victims were found with burns all over their body. The exact source of the burns was not known. Now he knew exactly what had occurred. Their abductors basically roasted them to death in the sauna. That was the fate that awaited him if he didn't escape. And that was something he would do anything to prevent.

Stephen Campana

Chapter 8

Adam rang the bell of the Gallo residence and waited. He was thirty minutes early. The meeting with Nick was for 7:00 PM. It was six thirty. He hoped he wasn't interrupting dinner. He felt awkward, standing there on this televangelist's front porch. He had always felt awkward around Christians, especially those of the born-again variety — the kind that felt the need to share their faith, as if they had a secret they just had to let you in on. *Hey, good news: Jesus loves you. He died for your sins and wants to save you; just accept Him so He won't have to torture you forever in hell.* It was all such bullshit. It did not offend him, though, as it did some people he knew, especially his Jewish friends. That's because he simply did not take these people seriously. To him, they were simply deluded at best, and mentally ill at worst. He felt no more offended by their need to "save" him than he did by a mental patient's need to warn him about little green men.

Cassie opened the door. "Hi, you must be Adam," she said, smiling. "Come in."

"Thank you," he said, returning the smile. He was struck by the woman's good looks.

"Nick will be down in a few minutes," she said,

gesturing him toward the sofa. "Have a seat." He thanked her and sat down.

"You have a lovely home, here," he said.

It was lovely, indeed. High ceilings, elegant décor, plush rugs, walls and shelves filled with tasteful paintings and photos. On the wall facing them, in stenciled letters, was the biblical phrase: *His mercy endures forever*. On the bookshelf, and on the coffee table, were a variety of Christian themed books, bibles, commentaries, and concordances. Pretty much what you would expect in the home of a Christian pastor. It would have made most people he knew — his Jew friends and his atheist friends — a tad uncomfortable. But not him. Their religious faith was their own business; it said nothing about him. Anyway, he liked the place. It was comfortable, but not opulent; classy, but not pretentious.

"Thank you," she said, in response to his compliment, and sat down in a chair just across from him, about five feet away. She was wearing a white blouse with a black knee-length skirt and a pair of low heel black shoes. She crossed her legs, revealing just a hint of thigh. His eyes locked on her legs for a moment — a rather long moment — and then darted back to her face, where they belonged. If she had noticed, she seemed not to mind. He felt strangely attracted to this woman, despite a substantial difference in age. And he sensed that she felt something as well.

"So," Adam said, "did your husband tell you why I'm here?"

He had assumed he did; from what he understood, she played an active role in their ministry, and frequently spoke from the pulpit on their weekly TV show *Listening to God*. "Yes," she said, "he did. He did." She paused for a moment, as if unsure of what to say next, then said: "So, you think one of your patients might be possessed?"

"Well," Adam said, "I personally don't believe so, but I think *he* thinks he is."

"Right," Cassie replied, nodding noncommittally. She seemed strangely hesitant, almost as if the subject of demonic possession seemed as silly to her as it did to him. In the course of his young career, Adam had counseled dozens — perhaps hundreds — of clergy people and family of clergy people, and found, more often than not, the public persona did not match the person's private thoughts and feelings. He got the sense that this was the case with Cassie. He did not think Cassie Gallo, loyal wife and faithful partner in Sword of the Spirit Ministries, was the *real* Cassie Gallo. There was something else there, seething just beneath the surface. Something that had been kept down for a long time. And right now, that something, that bottled energy, seemed to be taking the form of a sexual tension between the two of them. It seemed to be seeping out of her, like steam out of a leaky valve. And, frankly, he found it exciting.

"So, what exactly do you want to accomplish with an exorcism?" she asked, knitting her hands around her knee — the one attached to the leg that revealed the trace of thigh that Adam kept sneaking furtive glances at.

"Well, he said…."

"Oh, I'm sorry," she interrupted, "Where are my manners? Can I offer you something to drink?"

Surprised, Adam asked: "You mean, like alcohol?"

Cassie smiled a playful, almost motherly smile. "You mean I'm not allowed to have alcohol in my house," she said, furrowing her brow at him. She looked absolutely beautiful when she did that.

"No, no," he laughed, a little embarrassed. "I just

thought that Christians…I mean *devout* Christians….”

“Stop, stop!” she said, waving her hand. “I know what you meant; no explanation necessary.” She stood up and took two steps toward him. Then, with that motherly smile, she looked down at him and said, “You thought that devout Christians aren’t supposed to drink, right?”

Then she turned around and walked into the kitchen, which was just off the living room. She kept talking as she walked. “I guess that’s about the size of it,” Adam replied, somehow feeling very childish and embarrassed. He didn’t know why.

“Well, you’re right,” she said from the kitchen, as she fetched some glasses. “We really *aren’t* supposed to drink, but sometimes we do anyway.”

“Okay,” Adam laughed.

Then Cassie stood in the doorway that joined the living area and the kitchen. She held a bottle of Coke in one hand and a bottle of wine in the other. “You can have this,” she asked, holding up the soda, “Or….” Her voice grew hushed and solemn: “You can have this,” she said, holding up the wine.

“Which one are you having?” Adam asked.

“Why, the soda, of course,” she said, giving him that look again. “The wine is just for guests.”

He laughed. She was a funny lady. He liked that. “Make it two Cokes,” he said.

“Two Cokes coming up,” she replied.

Moments later, she popped back into the living room, handed him his glass, and sat back down. Only this time she did not sit across from him; she sat next to him on the sofa, and placed her Coke on the coffee table. Then she looked at him and said, “So…where were we?”

Adam looked at her as she crossed her legs again. She

crossed the one closest him over the other, affording him with a bird's eye view of the thigh he had been peaking at for the last several minutes. "Well...you asked me about the benefit of an exorcism for someone that I don't really believe is possessed."

"Right," she said. He detected an almost bemused quality to her voice. It was not intentional, he knew that, but it was there nonetheless, and it spoke volumes to him. Years of training had taught him how to read people. People were like walking polygraphs; they gave off signals all the time. By the way they moved, by their posture, by how often they blinked, by the inflections in their voice, by their use of their hands, and by a thousand other signals. A well-trained psychiatrist could read people; an intuitive one could read them even better. And he was intuitive. He felt like she was playing a role.

"Anyhow," he said, "the reason I think it might be—" He stopped himself in mid-sentence. He had the feeling that he was being humored, and decided to find out for sure. He looked Cassie right in the eyes and said, "You don't believe any of this stuff, do you? Be honest: you're just playing a role, aren't you?"

Cassie didn't know what to say. She was clearly taken aback. She just stared at Adam, as if to say: *How did you know that*? And in that moment, as their eyes met, there was a connection. Something passed between them, and they allowed themselves to stare at each other for much longer than was appropriate.

Just then, Nick came ambling down the stairs. Feeling as if he had been caught in something, Adam almost leapt out of his seat. "Hello, Mr. Gallo," he said, extending a hand.

"Please, call me Nick," Nick smiled, shaking Adam's

hand.

"Nice to meet you, Nick," Adam said.

"The same here," Nick replied, sitting down in the chair that Cassie had vacated moments ago.

"Well," Cassie said, standing up, "Maybe I should let you two alone to discuss…. Whatever it is you have to discuss."

"As you wish, dear," Nick said with a smile. "I'll see you later."

She smiled at Adam and said, "It was very nice meeting you."

"Nice meeting you, too," he said as she left the room. Then he looked at Nick and smiled, hoping he did not look as guilty as he felt. "I want to start off by thanking you for agreeing to meet with me," Adam said.

"Oh, you're quite welcome," Nick said. "I only hope I can be of assistance."

He sensed that Nick meant what he said. He got a good vibe from this man. "Oh, I believe you can," Adam responded. "As I said over the phone, I have a patient; his name is Martin Monroe, who believes he is possessed by a demon."

"Go on," Nick said.

"Well, I'll be honest with you," Adam said. "I personally do not believe he is possessed. In fact, I don't believe in demon possession at all."

When Nick showed no response, Adam decided to lay his cards on the table. "In fact," he said, "I don't even believe in God."

Again, Nick showed no response. This did not surprise Adam too much. In a way, he and Nick were a lot alike. They both listened to people spill their guts. He supposed that Nick, like himself, had learned to listen without judgment.

"It might surprise you to know," Nick said, "that until last week, neither did I." Adam listened as Nick recounted to him the incident at the Cockers house.

"Fascinating," Adam said simply.

"Thing is," Nick said, "when I first began my ministry, I *did* believe in possession. But gradually, I began to believe that these people were probably just sick. Mentally ill. But by then, well...." He paused, and sighed. "By then I was a professional exorcist. That was my thing. It was what people expected; it was what I did. So I kept doing it. And besides, I *did* feel like I was performing a service. These people did seem to get better."

"The placebo effect," Adam said.

"Exactly," Nick said.

"But after the murders the other night, well...." He paused. "I felt something in that house, even on my way to that house, that I had never felt before. Pure evil." He shook his head. "I don't expect you to believe me. Hell, until last week, *I* wouldn't have believed me. But what I felt.... That was real."

"Well," Adam said with a shrug, "I don't know what you felt out there, but I do know what I feel when I'm around this patient. I feel fear. I feel hopelessness. And I feel desperation. This man truly believes he is possessed. He truly believes an exorcism might help him. And he has requested you by name to be that exorcist."

"I guess I should be flattered," Nick said, smiling.

Adam returned the smile. "I guess you should. There's only one thing: My supervisor, the hospital administrator, is leery about this whole process."

"Quite understandable," Nick said.

"Yes," Adam replied. "He requested that the first time

you meet with Martin, that the meeting take more the form of an assessment. You know, get a feel for what we're dealing with, form some impressions, then sort of take it from there."

"No holy water and incantations the first time," Nick added.

"Exactly," Adam smiled.

"I understand completely," Nick said.

"Great," Adam said. "Well…then I guess the best way to proceed is…I will consult my supervisor and arrange for a meeting between you and Martin."

"That sounds fine," Nick said.

Adam stood up and shook Nick's hand. "I really want to thank you for this. I know you are a very busy man."

"We're all busy these days," Nick replied. "But the day we get too busy to help our fellow man…. Well, that's a sad day indeed."

Adam smiled. "Well put," he said.

On that note, Adam left. He left feeling a lot better about Nick than he felt before meeting him. And, of course, about his wife, too.

Chapter 9

Samantha felt very alone. Alone and bored. She had agreed to help Austin—*wanted* to help him—on this mission of his, but she did not count on the boredom and the loneliness. As a self-employed computer operator, she worked from home, and did not get out much. But it had become even worse since she and Austin had embarked upon this crusade. She couldn't have company, not even family. She had no social life at all. In fact, she felt like a full-time babysitter for whoever happened to be chained in the basement at the time.

But not only that. She was confused, too. Sometimes she understood the mission, sometimes it made perfect sense, and other times, it seemed pointless. Sometimes Austin seemed like a true Crusader, daring to stand up to a corrupt and tyrannical institution, and, in so doing, to help lead the world into a new era of expanded consciousness and unity. Other times he seemed no different than David Koresh or Charles Manson—just another deluded killer putting a religious spin on his crimes.

Even her own motives were a source of confusion to

her. Was she doing this out of commitment to a cause that she shared with Austin? Or simply out of a commitment to Austin himself, and a desire to be around him? And what about her desire for Austin? She loved him—always had and always would. She loved him with an everlasting love. In fact, he was the only person she had ever loved, or ever could love. But their relationship was strained, to say the least. To have sex with him, she had to wear wigs, speak in a different voice, sometimes even answer to a different name. It was an ongoing game of role-playing and fantasy that she was getting tired of playing. They rarely even had sex anymore, and when they did, it was not satisfying.

But then what did she expect? Austin was, after all, her brother. From the time they were children, when their father forced them to do things to each other, their relationship was a grotesque mixture of taboo and titillation, of seduction and sin, of sex and subterfuge. They could make no sense of it then, and they could make no sense of it now.

For Austin, the answer was to disassociate. His personality had fractured into two—maybe more—pieces. He was one person with her, another person in his daily life. And he didn't know it. He was a schizoid. A multiple personality. A wacko. And yet in some ways he was healthier than her. Their abusive past had left them both stunted, traumatized, and riddled with guilt. They both struggled with who they were and who they should be. But at least he had moved forward and forged a real life for himself. At least he had managed to escape from the dark forest of their sick and sordid past into the open pastures of a real life. A real life that was a lie, perhaps. One that hung by a slender thread over the raging fires of a past that constantly threatened to singe it in two, yes, but a real life all the same. One that, at the very least, did not revolve around her.

She, on the other hand, never could find another love — not even a reasonable facsimile. He was her first love, and, until this day, her only one. The bizarre and illicit bond they had forged in the fires of their twisted childhood had formed a hold on her that she could never break. No-one could ever understand her the way Austin did. No-one could ever love her the way he did. No-one could ever protect her the way he did. This was how it was; this is how it had to be. And if she could never have all of him, she would take some of him. If she could never have him whole, as a fully integrated personality, she would take half of him — the half that still loved and needed her like she loved and needed him. That was enough for now. It would have to be.

She got up from the couch and walked into the kitchen. She fetched some dishes from the cupboards and placed them on the table. Then she opened the fridge, took out some tuna fish and a can of mayo, and placed them next to the dishes. Next, she put two slices of bread on each dish. "God, I'm hungry," she muttered as she prepared two sandwiches, one on each dish. She picked one up and headed for the cellar door, which was just off to the left of the entrance to the kitchen. *Time to feed the prisoner.*

She walked slowly down the steps and toward the sauna room door. Before entering, she peered through a peephole Austin had put in the door for safety reasons. He didn't want her entering that room until she knew for sure their prisoner was safely contained. Looking through the peephole, she could see that he was right where they had left him, sitting on the bench, wrist chained to the pipe. *Good little prisoner,* she thought, throwing back the slide bolt and opening the large wooden door. Standing in the doorway, she knelt down, placed the plate on the floor, and slid it over to him.

He just sat there staring at her with sad, pleading eyes. It was getting hot in there. She wouldn't want to be in his shoes right now. She stared back at him for a moment, then shut the door. *Pretty soon, I'm going to have to start having some fun with you.* Already, she had some ideas. Austin wouldn't approve. He did not want her to take any unnecessary risks, but that was okay. She would be careful. A girl had to have some fun.

Chapter 10

Nick walked through the large glass doors of the Riverview Mental Hospital and stopped at the reception desk. From behind the counter, the security guard—an elderly black man with glasses and a bald head—peered at him from behind a newspaper. The man smiled, revealing a set of pearly white teeth that might or might not have been his own. "Can I help you?" the guard asked pleasantly.

"I'm here to see Martin Monroe," Nick said.

The man looked at his computer, punched in a few digits, and said, "Room 202," handing him a visitor's pass.

"Thank you," Nick said with a smile. The man wished him a nice day as Nick headed for the lobby elevator. He stepped in, pressed 2, and waited. Two young orderlies stepped in behind him. One was thin, with glasses, and her hair in a bun; the other was heavy, with too much make-up, and a weird, sour look on her face. Neither looked too happy to be there.

He soon found out why. As he walked down the corridor, checking the room numbers as he went, Nick could tell Riverview was not one of your finer mental health facilities. State-run institutions seldom were. As a pastor, he had visited his share of hospitals—regular hospitals, mental hospitals, veterans' hospitals, children's hospitals, rehabs, hospices—and he had a pretty good sense about them. And this one was the pits.

As he passed by the rooms, he could see patients from the corner of his eyes. He could hear them, too—and the awful sounds they made were enough to make his blood curdle. Most of the people here were old and sick looking, probably dumped there by family members too poor to afford a decent retirement home.

As he strode down the hallway, he began to experience a strange, yet familiar sensation. It was the one he had experienced a week ago as he neared the Cockers's home. It was that same exact feeling of dread, that same sense of a fist tightening around him. And suddenly he felt almost sure that Adam was wrong. This was not merely a case of mental illness. This was not merely a guilt-ridden man inventing his own demon. No, this was the real thing.

His heart began beating faster, just as it did at the Cockers's house. He turned a corner and kept walking as the room numbers got closer and closer to 202. He could see Adam standing outside of Martin's room in the hallway, where he had told Nick he would meet him. The closer he got the stronger the feeling grew—the feeling of a presence, hanging thick in the air, like a mist. By the time he reached Martin's room, he could actually *smell* it. It smelled like a corpse—only worse.

He shook hands with Adam. The two men had discussed how to proceed. At Monroe's insistence, no-one would be present during this meeting—just himself and Nick. "How's our patient feeling today?" Nick asked, trying not to sound a lot more relaxed than he felt.

"Unusually subdued," Adam said. "I think he is really looking forward to meeting you. And so is his...other personality."

"You mean the demon," Nick said.

"Correct. One seems eager for you to help him. The other is eager to...well...confront you."

"Yes," Nick said. His voice must have betrayed his apprehension because Adam immediately jumped in and said: "But remember, they are the same person. It's all just Martin Monroe."

If Nick wasn't sure that Adam was wrong before, he was sure now. The feeling that hung in the air, just outside that room, told him for sure that it wasn't just a person in there. It was a person and a *presence*. "Thank you, doctor," Nick said.

"I'll see you in a bit," Adam replied, patting Nick on the shoulder as he walked away. Nick watched as he ambled down the long corridor, leaving him there, alone, outside the door. He looked through the glass window on the door, into Martin's room. He could see very little of the man; he was tucked away under several layers of white bedding. His face was at an angle, tucked into his shoulder. *Trying to hide, perhaps? Playing a game of possum?*

Nick put a sweaty hand on the door knob and turned. Slowly, he walked into the room. "Hello, Martin," he said, approaching the foot of the bed. The smell of death was strong in the air. And this death smelled like hatred—a hatred as pure and raw and undiluted as anything anyone had ever experienced. It was the hatred that remained like a film on one's soul, after everything else had been drained out. A slimy, rotting, mossy, green film. That's what this thing was; it was what was *left* when everything good was gone. It was absence given a presence; a void given form; a shadow given substance. It was death given...not life, no. Existence. It was death propped up and given a face. That's what that thing inside of Martin was. And right now, standing there at his bedside, Nick could smell it. And it made him want to retch.

He moved in for a closer look, standing by the side of the bed. He looked down at the sleeping patient. He did not want to wake him. There was an energy radiating out of him, like heat from the body of someone in the grip of 106 degree fever. He could feel it, he could smell it, he could almost see it. It seemed almost impossible to him that no-one else did. Then again, Nick was sensitive to these things. He always had been; it was a gift. And also, sometimes, a curse.

He drew up a chair and sat down by bed. Then he bent forward, his face almost touching the bed-rail, and took a closer look at the man's face. He was about forty. Deep lines creased his pallid cheeks. His thinning hair was matted and stringy, and the top of his head seemed too big for his gaunt, sunken face. Nick stood back up. He needed a drink of water. There was a tray by the bed with a pitcher and some paper cups. With his back to Martin, he steadied his hands and very slowly started pouring himself a cup of water. As he did, he was thinking— almost praying: *Just let him sleep through this. Just let him stay asleep. I can just go home and tell Adam I didn't want to wake him.*

"Hellooooo, Nick," a deep, guttural voice sounded from just behind him in the bed. Nick dropped the water and turned around hurriedly, as if to defend himself from an attacker. There was no attacker—just Martin Monroe, laughing at him through two rows of crooked, rotting teeth. His eyes, dead and gray, bulged in their sockets. He looked like some kind of talking Halloween skull.

Nick just stood there, transfixed. His heart was racing. For one long awful moment, he thought he would actually flee. He could almost feel his legs make a move, independently of his brain, for the door. But he didn't. Instead, he simply turned around, his back to Martin, and started cleaning up the spilled water with paper towels. He wanted—he *needed*—a moment to gather his composure. As he did, Martin just continued laughing. The laughter got lower and deeper, until it faded off completely.

Nick did not like to be laughed at. He began to feel his fear giving way to anger. And shame. A "demon hunter" all these years, he finally encounters the real thing and wants to run away like a frightened child.

He took a deep breath and turned around to face Martin—or the Thing that was inside of him. It said, "Please, sit down," gesturing toward the chair. Its voice sounded like the creak of a rusty old hinge. Nick obliged and sat back down. The Thing smiled at him and said, "We have so much to talk about, you and me."

Nick did not want to talk. He only wanted to drive that thing out of Martin. But he had promised Adam he would not attempt that today. Today was a "consultation."

"What do you want with Martin?" Nick asked.

"Oh, how rude," the Thing replied. "I am trying to be a gracious host, but all you can think about is getting rid of me." The Thing looked around, a sneer of disproval on his lips, then said, "It is too bright in here, don't you think? There is no...." He looked around the room, his head swiveling loosely on his pencil like neck, as if the right word to finish his sentence might be hiding in a corner. "Ambience," he said.

A moment later the lights went out, except for one dim, fluorescent bulb in the ceiling panels just above them. Now bathed in a dim light, the Thing's boney, pale face took on the look of a jack-o-lantern sitting in a window. He smiled again and said, "That's better." As Nick looked at the grotesque visage before him, he suddenly realized that he had seen it—seen Martin—before. He searched his mind, trying to recall when. "You recognize me, don't you?" the Thing asked, amused by Nick's memory lapse.

"Yes, I do," Nick replied. "Not you. I recognize Martin."

"Oh, but I have been *in* Martin for a long time," the Thing declared with obvious satisfaction. Nick searched his memory banks, but could not recall. The Thing laughed its slow creaking door laugh and asked, "Do you *want* to remember?"

"Yes," Nick said.

Another creak. "Very well. I will tell you…. In your dreams."

"No, I want to know now," Nick said.

Then, without warning, the Thing's face hardened into an angry sneer; the veins in his neck began to throb and pulsate, like snakes trying to break through his flesh, and a thin mist of smoke flowed through the pores of his skin, like an overheating pipe valve. When he spoke, it was with a voice that quivered with rage and sounded like thunder. The sound surrounded Nick, as if it were coming from every angle, and his ears split with pain from the volume. "You putrid little worm!" the Thing hollered. "Do you think you could challenge me? Investigate me? Plumb my depths? You have existed for a nano-second on this sliver of rock called earth and you dare to challenge one who walked with God in Eden and tread entire worlds like stones in a pond? You filthy, vile, little speck of dust!"

The Thing's voice was so loud that it actually hurt Nick's ears, and he recoiled in pain. He took a moment to compose himself, then simply stared at the demon and then, quoting from Scripture, he said: "Know ye not that we shall *judge angels*?"

The Thing said nothing for a moment. Then, slowly, its lips curled into an angry sneer, and it sat up in bed, staring at Nick. A brief moment passed and then it lunged forward and unleashed a massive blast of hot, almost scalding breath from its mouth. It hit Nick like heat from a busted steam pipe. He fell backward, off his chair, and onto the floor. As he scrambled to his feet, the Thing kept up the attack, keeping the blast of air locked on him. It knocked him into the wall and pinned him there. Nick howled with pain. To make matters worse, the heat was accompanied by what had to be the most loathsome, fetid stench ever produced. It smelled like something dredged up from the deepest bowels of hell. Nick prayed for it to pass, and then, after what seemed like minutes, but was only seconds, it did.

The assault ceased. Nick crumpled to his knees, hands covering his singed eyes, then gagged violently. Nothing came up; he had not eaten in hours. He just sat there, kneeling, for several more moments. When he stood up again, the Thing was gone, and in its place lay Martin Monroe, his hand outstretched. "Help me, Pastor Gallo," he pleaded, his eyes full of fear and despair.

Nick took a large gulp of air. "I will, my son," he said, taking the man's hand and standing by his side. "I will."

Stephen Campana

Chapter 11

Samantha looked up at the sign overhead the small shop, which was neatly nestled in between a Jewish deli and a pizza place. It read simply: *Sophie's Sex Toys*. She opened the door and walked in. Off to the side of the entrance was a large glass counter with a man standing behind it looking at a newspaper. He was bald, with a big belly, a grey goatee, and a cigar nub in his mouth that he appeared to be chewing rather than smoking. He had a suspicious look about him that made Sam uncomfortable.

It was a small place, with every available inch of space jam-packed with stuff, and very little room to move. Slowly, she made her way through the place, examining the merchandise. Everywhere were mannequins fitted in various kinds of attire; glass cases full of exotic shoes; slinky underwear on hangers on the walls; shelves full of X-rated films, vibrators, dildos, condoms, whips, chains, and other assorted sexual delicacies.

It was the S & M stuff that interested her, though. As she surveyed the choices, she could see the guy behind the counter stealing quick, furtive glances at her, then planting his eyes back in his paper. She couldn't decide if he was checking her out or if he was just suspicious. She waited for a moment, caught his next glance, and gave him a tiny little wave and a smile. He put the paper down and came out from behind the counter. He had the top three buttons of his shirt open, revealing a hairy chest and a silver necklace with a locket on the end. He smiled as he approached. Taking the cigar nub out his mouth, he said: "Can I help you, ma'am?"

"Well," Sam said, looking at him from the corner of her eye, "maybe you can."

The man chuckled lightly and said, "Well, that's what I'm here for." He waited for a moment. When she didn't respond, he said, "What are you looking for?"

"Well," Sam said, speaking slowly and deliberately, "I have someone that I want to…*punish*."

"Ah, punishment," the man said, sticking the nub back in his mouth. "Well, at Sophie's we're all about punishment." Somehow, the cigar in his mouth did not impede his speech at all. "Come over here, let me show you what we've got." He steered her gently by the elbow. "I find it best to dress a woman from the feet up. So let's start with the shoes." He sounded like a used car salesman giving a pitch he had given a thousand times before, and yet, somehow, still enjoying it.

He brought her to a glass case filled with shoes and spread his hands out. "All right, let me ask you…. Do you like high heels?"

Looking at the case, she smiled and said, "Hmmm…I don't know? Do I like high heels?"

He looked down at her shoes, taking the opportunity to give her a once over. "Well, you're not wearing them now, but I'm gonna say you're the kind of lady who likes to slap those spikes on every now and then. Am I right?"

He leaned in, smiling broadly. She thought he was deriving an absurd amount of pleasure out of this. It was really kind of pathetic. "I guess," she said, putting a finger on her lips as she tried to decide between all those shoes. High-heel shoes. Low-heel shoes. Thigh-high shoes. Suede shoes. Leather shoes. Shoes with spikes protruding all over the place. Shoes with three straps covering the feet; shoes with two straps; shoes with one strap. Shoes with spikes coming out of the straps. Shoes with ankle straps. Etc....

"Let me ask you something," the man said in a near whisper, leaning in and touching her elbow. "Who is this guy you want to punish?"

She kept looking at the shoes as she answered. "Oh, he's just...a guy. You know, they're all the same, right?"

"Well," he said, his voice even lower. "Has he been a really bad boy?"

"Oh, yes," she said.

"I mean...do you want to really hurt him?"

She looked right at the man, her mouth inches from his, and said softly, "I want to *kill* him."

The man's eyes widened with surprise, and he let out a small gasp. Then he smiled slyly and said, "I love a woman who means business."

Over the next fifteen minutes, he gave her a guided tour through the merchandise, helping her with each selection. Shoes, bras, panties, bustier, whips, chains, gloves, and a mask. Five hundred dollars later, she thanked him and went on her way.

****

As soon as Sam got home, she ran into her bedroom, and dumped the contents of her bags onto the bed. Then she laid it all out on the bed so she could get a good look at her brand new purchases. This was exciting. She had never bought anything like this before. In fact, she had never even experimented with S & M before. What would she look like as a Dominatrix? And what exactly would she *do* to him? She had no idea. That's why she had purchased several bondage DVDs — to get some ideas. After all, she wanted this to be *fun*. At this point in her life, she owed herself some fun. Up until now her life had been anything but fun. It had been about survival and not much else. And she was good at that — at surviving. Surviving and doing whatever she had to do to get by. She had never been afraid of hard work. And that's what her life for the past twenty years had been about — hard work and survival.

She left home at eighteen and worked odd jobs to put herself through night school, where she learned computer operating. Upon graduation she secured an entry-level job with a reputable firm. She worked there for two decades. She put in long hours and received regular promotions and good pay. She got up, went to work, came home, went to sleep. And for the past twenty years, that was pretty much her whole life. No social life. No men. No friends. Oh, she had tried from time to time, but it never worked out. She trusted no-one. No-one except Austin. And he had managed to eek out his own life. A real life with real people. But he still made time for her. He still saw her regularly, and they still had a relationship. Yes, even a sexual relationship. No-one suspected, of course. They just assumed he was just visiting his dear younger sister. No harm in that. And that was basically the life she had lived for the last twenty years.

Until he had his vision. Until he decided he had to go on this crusade and that he wanted her to help. So she did.

She did not know where it was going—to their destruction, probably—but she did know it didn't really matter. She had a purpose now. She had *him* now. If it all ended in flames in a few months, it didn't really matter. What would she lose? Nothing.

She looked at the clothes laid out on the bed. It gave her a strange surge of excitement. A tingling, almost. It was nothing fancy; just the basics: a bustier, stockings, garters, and a pair of high-heel boots. All black. She liked black; it was her favorite color. Also on the bed were two S & M DVDs. One was titled *Hurt so good*; the other *Insane Pain*. Both featured men tied up, naked, and under the heels of dominatrixes. Sexual domination. She liked the idea; wondered why it had not occurred to her sooner. Isn't that precisely what she had been subjected to? And by her preacher father no less? Now, the roles would be reversed. She would torture the preacher. Of course, Austin didn't know what she was up to; he would not approve. He didn't want her to take any unnecessary risks. Nothing that could jeopardize the mission. She did not feel comfortable going behind his back this way. What if something *did* go wrong? What if she really was jeopardizing the mission?

She tried not to think about it. For now, all she was doing was trying on some clothes. No harm in that. Austin wouldn't like it, but then Austin didn't have to find out. Suddenly, she felt strangely self-conscious as she stood there, preparing to try on the clothes on the bed. She looked around the room, as if to make sure she was alone. *Maybe I should check on him*, she thought. What if he got loose while I was out? He could be lurking behind the door for all I know. A slight chill ran up her spine. She left the bedroom, walked down the stairs, and headed straight for the basement. She bounded down the stairs, suddenly in a hurry to make sure the prisoner was still there. Sweating, she stopped at the large, wooden door and peaked in. There he was, just as she had left him — chained to the pipe.

She breathed a sigh of relief and ran back up the stairs, anxious now to try on her new clothes. As she entered the bedroom, she was already pulling her blouse over her head. She dumped it on the floor, then slid off her shoes and wriggled out of her jeans. Next she unhitched her bra and tossed that on a chair. Then she pulled down her panties, letting them drop at her bare feet. She stood there, naked, before the bed, and took a big gulp of air. This was strangely exciting — even arousing. She began to feel wet between her legs, and placed a hand there. She rubbed just a little, more as if scratching an itch than trying to get herself off, then picked up the first item of clothing on her bed — the bustier. She had never worn one of these before. Standing before the full length closet mirror, she held it up to her chest, posed for a moment, then put it on. She had some trouble cinching it up in back, but after some wrestling, she managed. She looked at herself in the mirror, standing there naked except for a tight, black bustier. She cupped her breasts and pushed up, giving herself a little lift. *Not bad for an older woman* she thought. She found herself smiling wryly — wickedly, almost — as she admired herself in the four foot frame of rectangular glass that reflected her image back to her.

Next, she picked up the panties — lacy, black, skimpy — and slid slowly, seductively, into them, as if putting on a show for herself. Which, she supposed, she was. Again, she stood before the mirror, hands on her hips, turning one way, then the next, admiring herself.

You sexy thing, she thought. She almost *wished* someone were spying on her. Maybe some teenage boy, hands on his nuts, eying her from across the street through a telescope, like something out of a Hitchcock movie. Just the thought was making her wetter and wetter down there. Again, she rubbed her crotch, this time watching herself in the mirror as she did so.

Next she sat on the bed and grabbed the black nylon stockings. She rolled them up, slipping a toe in the foot, then slowly unrolled it up one leg. Then she did the same for the other leg. She put her hands on her hips, then slid them slowly down her legs, caressing the smooth nylon fabric. *Bet that teen in the window's just about to blow his load.*

She slipped on the black boots, attached the garters from her panties to her bustier, and presto, the transformation was complete. In a matter of minutes, she had gone from humble Suburban computer operator to Mistress Samantha; Dominatrix Supreme. She grabbed the long, black leather whip from the bed and stood before the mirror, her feet in a wide stance, toes pointed slightly outward. She snapped the whip against the floor, loving the feeling. She now understood why people got so into this stuff. She snapped it again, as her lips curled into a sneer. Oh, yeah, this was fun. Again she snapped it — once, twice, three more times. *Go ahead teen boy; blow your load NOW, go, go, go.... Oh yeaaaahhh!*

Sweating, she took off the bustier and the boots. Then she took one of the DVDs — *Hurt So Good* — and slid it into the DVD player. Then she hopped onto the bed and pulled the sheets up over her naked body. On the screen a woman dressed in a negligee scolded a man for spilling his drink. The man apologized profusely, but to no avail. Within minutes he was on all fours, his hands and feet bound, as the woman, who went by the moniker Mistress X, put a heel on his back and slapped his ass hard with her hand. His dick hung down between his legs like a giant sausage. He looked like a dog in heat.

She slid her panties off. Then she slid her hand under the covers, down her belly, and between her legs. She was already moist as she slipped two fingers inside of herself. She let out a moan as she messaged her clitoris. Already she was starting to feel like she might come. She pinched her nipple with her free hand, then started messaging it gently. The man on the screen's butt was slowly turning a bright red from the spanking. His cries for mercy really turned her on. Each cry, each whimper, each gasp, brought her a little bit closer to climax. She closed her eyes and began fingering herself furiously.

She was grateful to be alone in the house, as she could make all the noise she pleased. And she could tell this was going to be a *very* noisy one. So much had been building up for so long. *Ohhhhhhh*, she gasped, her fingers buried in the hairy mound of moist, throbbing flesh between her glistening, perfectly shaped thighs. Her knees began to lift, almost involuntarily, toward her chest, as her back arched and her body began to stiffen. *Ohhhhhhhh, yeah,* she gasped, as she spread her legs out wide. She could feel it now; she was just about there. A few more strokes and she would be ready to come. She wanted to time it perfectly. It was like catching a wave; start a second — even a split second — too early or too late and you ruin the whole thing. But hit it just right and.... Wow!

So she held herself. Although she desperately wanted to finish, she held herself, waiting for just the right moment. This was the hardest part — the waiting. The timing. *Ohhhhhhh, yeah,* she gasped, her face contorting into a mask of what looked almost like pain, but was really intense pleasure. Intense pleasure escalating into almost unbearable pleasure. She did not know until now how much pain could turn her on. Didn't know until she heard the desperate, anguished whimpering of that poor pathetic wretch under the heel of that woman, where he so truly belonged. God, it turned her on. She could not believe how much; she could not believe the intensity of the feeling building between her legs, and reverberating throughout her body. For a brief moment she almost wondered if she could *handle* it.

She could hold out no longer. She was coming. She was coming fast and hard. Her fingers moved inside of her soaking wet bush like pistons. The air smelled of sweat and sex. Her back arched, and her toes curled as the wave of pleasure reached its apex. *Ohhhhhhhhhh God*! she gasped, spreading her legs even wider, her toes pointing up toward the ceiling.

Usually she came fast and it was over. The wave would roll in, sweeping her up in a flood of pleasure. Then it would roll back out, like the tide after soaking the beach with its waves. But not this time. This time there was another wave coming right behind the first. And this one, unbelievably, was even stronger — perhaps because it was unexpected. Gasping, she braced herself for another one. Her face was a mask of contorted pleasure. *Ohhhhhhhhhh God*! she almost screamed. Her voice had a desperate, pleading quality, as if she just wanted it to be over — to experience the release of tension and then lay back and relax.

But it would not be that easy. To her absolute, utter amazement, a third even bigger wave was on the way. By this time she felt almost as if some alien force had seized control of her body, imprisoning her in wave after wave of convulsive pleasure. She had never ever experienced anything remotely like this before. She was almost crying as the third wave rolled in. It was stronger than the last one. Her entire body stiffened like a board; her back arched so hard it hurt. She let out a gasp of pain, closing her eyes and fingering furiously, almost angrily, as if trying to expel something. As the third wave overtook her, she felt a sudden intense pressure in her abdominal area. For a moment, she felt as if she might explode. Then a gusher of thick, oozy fluid gushed out of her, spilling onto her fresh white linen.

But that was just the tip of the iceberg. After she came, she felt all of her abdominal muscles suddenly relax and she realized, to her horror, that she was about to pee the bed. She could not stop it, so she just laid back and let it come out—a big geyser of pee flowing out from between her legs onto the linen like water falling from a lake into a stream. The sensation of the pee pulsing through her throbbing pussy excited her. There was still a residual sexual energy in her body, even after that flood of release. That was unusual for her. Normally, after an orgasm she felt no trace of sexual excitement remaining; she just felt spent. But this time she still felt something. Even as she closed her eyes, exhausted and limp, she still felt aroused.

Her fingers were still between her legs. She rubbed some more. There was still some sensitivity. How could that be, after three orgasms? She didn't know. Maybe it was the video. This was a new experience for her and her body was responding in unexpected ways. She looked at the tape, mesmerized. The woman on the screen was torturing her victim. He lay on the floor, bound and gagged, as she tickled his butthole with a vibrator. *God, no,* she thought. She was becoming excited again. Very excited. She thought about simply stopping the tape, hopping out of bed, and jumping into the shower. But she didn't. Couldn't. Within seconds she was fingering herself again. The urine smelled strong. That's because it wasn't just piss; it was a potent mixture of urine and her vaginal juices that had built up and marinated for a long time before finally gushing out onto the bed. She watched, transfixed, as Mistress X taunted the poor wretch. She had discarded the vibrator and was licking at her victim's fully erect penis with her tongue. He squirmed around on the floor like a worm, bound and helpless, as his mistress tormented him with pleasure, then denial. Sam could almost see his dick throbbing, demanding release. It was not to be, however. Every time he got close, she brought her tongue back in her mouth, rolling it around the inside of her lips and cheeks. All the while her lips were curled in a devilish grin.

The woman turned her on as much as the man. More in fact. She was not particularly beautiful; nor that young. In fact she seemed almost miscast in the role. She looked more like a soccer mom than a Dominatrix. But that's what Sam found so appealing. She looked *real*. It was her face, her body that Sam had fixed on as she fingered herself. Within minutes, she felt that wave building again. She dug her feet into the bed, arched her back, and prepared to catch it at just the right moment. She moaned, her body on fire. *Ohhhhhh, God…. Ohhhhh.* She gasped for air, like a runner nearing the finish line of a marathon. Unbelievably, this one was even more intense than the last. Soaked in urine and sweat, her body convulsing, she prepared for another earth shattering flood of pleasure. As it came, she all but cried with pleasure, her face contorted horribly, like a woman in the throes of childbirth. And that is what this one felt like. It was a strange feeling, unlike anything she had ever experienced. It felt like she was trying to pass a thousand pounds of pleasure through one small, slim opening, and she was having trouble doing it. *Can an orgasm get stuck?* she wondered, now actually feeling a sense of trepidation.

But it wasn't just the sensation between her legs; there was also a pressure in her bladder and her colon. As she reached the edge, her whole body, it seemed, demanded release. She needed not only to cum, but to poop and pee as well, and somehow all three things were tied together. The pressure—and the pleasure—intensified. She *was* crying now; actual tears streamed down her cheeks, as her abdomen tightened. She was ready to explode, *needed* to explode, but could not. She stopped fingering and put her hands on her stomach, expecting that the sensations would cease. They didn't. She was suspended in *mid-orgasm,* unable to finish and unable to retreat, as if some alien force had seized control of her body, imprisoning her in a cocoon of intense sensations that she could not release.

Her eyes fixed on Mistress X. The woman lifted her head from the man's penis and looked at her audience. "Are you folks at home getting really horny?" she asked. "Maybe you need some help getting off?"

Sam was puzzled. What was this woman talking about? Mistress X looked at the man, his dick cinched up, his butthole plugged, and said, "Do you feel like him—all plugged up? Hmmm? Do you need my help?" She smiled wryly, like a mother talking to a naughty child. "Why don't you just ask? Say 'Mistress X, please help me.'"

Sam could not fathom what was going on, but she was

desperate. To her amazement, she found herself uttering the words: "Please help me."

"That's it," Mistress X cooed, "Don't be shy. Just ask. Ask and you *shall* receive." She spoke in a soft, hypnotic voice. "Go ahead," she continued. "Ask again."

"Please Mistress X," Sam said in a small, weak voice. "Help me."

"Good," Mistress X whispered, her face close to the screen now. She had a kind, pretty face, with full lips, bright green eyes, and a warm, sympathetic smile. "I *will* help you," she said, "but first, let me help this poor soul."

She looked down at the man. He lay on the floor on his back, hands and feet bound, legs up in the air, spread out, providing a full, frontal view of his butthole and his penis. She crawled over to him like a cat, placing one hand on the cinch around his dick and the other on the butt plug. He looked at her helplessly. "Are you ready?" she asked him.

"Yes, yes, Oh God, yes!" he gasped.

"Okay," she said…then paused. "Are you sure you can handle this?"

"Yes, yes, pleeeeease!"

She smiled wryly, caressing his belly with her palm. "Okay, then." She took the dick cinch between her forefinger and thumb with one hand, and with the other did the same with the butt plug. Then, after a moment's hesitation, gently removed both. As the man cried in relief, she hovered over him, face inches from his, then slowly brought her lips down to his own, and kissed him softly, muffling his moans of ecstasy. A massive geyser of cum shot out from his penis. At the same time his butthole stretched and a big brown turd slowly inched out. His entire body convulsed with uncontrollable pleasure.

Another load of cum followed. Then another. And another and another. All the while the massive turd, about an inch thick, pushed its way out.

Sam knew women could have multiple orgasms, but men? *That* many? It did not seem possible. What seemed to sustain him in that state, she thought, was her kiss. It seemed as if she were transmitting a kind of sexual energy through her mouth into his body. He began to squirm beneath her, almost as if he wanted her to *stop.* But she didn't. She kept kissing; kept him locked in this dizzying orgy of orgasmic ecstasy. Then, finally, she lifted her head and it was over. He breathed a huge sigh of relief. A moment later, a flood of pee came gushing out of his penis.

"Oh, that must have felt so good," Mistress X said, smiling into the camera. "Now…let's see what we can do for the rest of you guys…." She paused and smiled, then said "and *gals.*"

Sam couldn't take much more of this. Whatever magic this woman wielded, she needed it *now,* or else she would explode. "Now," Mistress X said, her face filling the screen, "what do you want me to do? Hmmm…?" After a moment of silence passed, she said, "Come on now; talk to me."

Sam found herself answering in spite of herself — in spite of knowing this woman couldn't really be talking to *her*. She said, "The same thing, do the same thing for me."

"The same thing?" Mistress X repeated "But…you're a woman."

Sam didn't understand. How did this person know who was talking to her? This was not possible. She said nothing. A few more moments passed and Mistress X said, "Sam, are you still with me?"

Sam was too addled to think, too excited to analyze. She just gave up and said, "Yes. Yes. I'm still here."

Mistress X smiled warmly. "Good," she said. "I thought I had lost you for a second there. Now.... What can I do for you?"

"You know what!" Sam gasped, "Please, just do it."

Mistress X replied in a soft, hypnotic voice, her glistening lips filling the screen. "Do you want me to...*kiss you*?" she asked. "Like I did with him?"

"Yes, yes, please," Sam answered.

Mistress X smiled and said, "All right, let's see what we can do." The camera panned out, and her whole body was now visible. Then she slipped one hand, palm turned outward, through the screen, and gripped the side of the television set. Then she did the same with the other hand and began slowly and carefully pulling herself through the TV set. Moments later, the celluloid image had disappeared and been replaced with a flesh and blood woman. A woman standing right there in her bedroom, at the foot of Sam's bed.

"Are we having some trouble here?" she asked, running a finger down Sam's lower leg.

"Yes," Sam pleaded, gasping. The pressure inside of her was almost unbearable. Mistress X gracefully sauntered over to the side of the bed. Sam's eyes traced her movement helplessly, her fingers still working inside of her. If she stopped it got worse, like an itch when you stopped scratching. She never felt so helpless, so small, in all her life. There she was, naked, in a pool of her own urine, desperately pleading with this perfect stranger to release her from the throes of this bizarre orgasmic suspension. It was utterly humiliating.

Mistress X took Sam's vibrator from her dresser and

looked at it impishly. "Hmmm…. This is a nice one," she said. She sat next to Sam on the bed. Her perfume was intoxicating, and her body threw off a pleasant warmth. It made Sam even more aroused, heightening her glorious agony. Sam knew what would end it — only one thing: the woman's kiss, just as it did for the man in the film. But pleading for a kiss; it seemed too much for her. Too degrading, too humiliating. She couldn't do it. At least not yet.

Mistress X placed the vibrator between Sam's legs, and turned it on, tickling her anal cavity. The tingling sensation caused a spasm inside her abdomen. She could feel her intestines pushing a humungous turd toward her rectum. She had never felt this kind of pressure before. Whatever was building up in there, and trying to push out, it was far bigger, far thicker than normal. She did not even think she *could* get it out.

She looked at Mistress X helplessly. The mistress returned the gaze. "You okay?" She smiled, then, without waiting for an answer, she tickled her anal hole some more.

"Ohhhhhhhh," Sam gasped, as the pressure in her intestines became almost unbearable. She was going. Right there in the bed; she was having a bowel movement. She raised her chin toward her chest and spread her legs, like a woman in labor. She shrieked with a mixture of agony and ecstasy as an incredibly warm fullness filled her rectum, like a giant, monstrous dick.

Mistress X gasped with mock surprise and her eyes widened as she looked at Sam and placed her head between Sam's legs for a closer look at her ass, gasped again, and said, looking at Sam, "Oh, my gosh!" Then she smiled and laughed. She put a hand to her mouth. "I don't mean to laugh; I've just never seen a grown woman shit in her own bed." She giggled again and put a hand on Sam's stomach. "Oh, I'm sorry. You poor dear. This must be so humiliating for you." She looked down at Sam, frowning.

Sam *did* feel humiliated, but that was not her primary concern right now. The Mistress began messaging her stomach. Her touch seemed to increase the pressure on Sam's intestines, helping to force the turd out. "Does that help?" the Mistress asked.

"Yes," Sam gasped.

"Yes, it does."

The Mistress took her hand off Sam's stomach, crossed her legs, and blew on her fingernails, as if suddenly disinterested in the whole situation. "You know," she said, "I could really use a manicure." Sam knew what was going on. The Mistress wanted to be begged. She had no choice but to play along.

Swallowing what little remained of her pride, she said, "Please, help. Put your hand back on my stomach."

"What's that, hon? I can't hear you." the Mistress replied, attending to her fingernails.

"Pleeeaasse!" Sam groaned.

"Look at me when you speak," the Mistress said.

Sam looked at her. "Please!" she begged.

"Well…I don't know," the Mistress said.

"Please! Please help me."

The Mistress smiled at her and said, "Okay." Then she resumed messaging her stomach.

"Ohhhhhh, thank you," Sam cried, as her bowels released. Mistress X had taken the liberty of sliding a pillow case under her to catch what came out. She scooped it up, opened the bedroom window, and tossed it out. "Thank you," Sam said, gasping. All pretense of pride was gone now; she had been stripped, literally and figuratively. She was naked before her mistress now — body and soul. As naked and helpless as anyone could be. It was not a bad feeling. In fact, it felt good. It turned her on.

Mistress X caressed Sam's hair. "Oh, you're welcome, sweetie." She smiled. "But you still need some more help, don't you?"

Panting, Sam looked up and her and gasped, "Yes, please. Please, help me!" Shivers of pleasure rippled through her body; her every nerve throbbed with a horrible bottled up ecstasy just crying for release. Her heart raced and a thick film of sweat covered her body from head to toe.

"Yeah," the Mistress said, running her slender, delicate fingers through Sam's sweat-soaked, matted mop of black hair. "You really do need help."

Her touch made it even worse, if possible, sending a thousand pricks of pleasure reverberating through her entire body. She was almost paralyzed, her muscles limp. Her fingers slid out of her pussy; she did not even have the strength to hold them up. Now her body was on fire with an itch that she couldn't even scratch.

She was crying now. Real tears. Streaming down her sweat-soaked face. "You poor dear," Mistress X said, cradling Sam's head and torso in her arms with one hand, and sliding the other between her legs. She gently caressed her pubic hairs. "Does that feel nice, hmmm?" she asked, looking down at Sam and smiling that warm motherly smile.

Defeated and helpless, Sam could only plead for what she needed. "Deeper," she begged. "Go deeper."

The mistress complied, sliding two fingers inside of

Sam. "Is that better?" she asked.

"Yeah," Sam cried. But it wasn't; not really. The woman's touch lit up her nerves with unbearable sensations of pleasure that demanded release. But that release, she knew, would not come from her touch down there. It would only come from her kiss. And for that, Sam knew, Mistress X wanted to be begged. Isn't that what domination was all about? Tease and denial? Torture? Of course it was. Sam had just never imagined it could occur on this kind of scale. Almost too weak to speak, Sam cried, "Kiss me."

Pretending not to hear, Mistress X continued fingering Sam. But now it was only making it worse. It was no longer like an itch being scratched. Instead it was like a fire being doused with gasoline. "Stop, please," Sam gasped. "Ohhhhhh, Stop, stop, stoooooopppppp!"

Mistress X obeyed. She kept the fingers in, but stopped moving them around. "What's the matter, hon?" she asked, cradling Sam's head and leaning forward, her red, glistening lips inches from Sam's own. "Are you okay?"

Sam could feel the woman's breath on her. She *had* to kiss her. Now. But she didn't even have the strength to move. In fact, she couldn't even speak. All she could do was lay there, naked, in her own urine, staring at the woman, and pleading with her eyes. *Kiss me, Kiss me, Kiss me PLEASE kiss me, oh God, please, please, please, please kiss me.*

The Mistress met her gaze, locking eyes with her, and then, slowly, brought her lips down towards Sam's, until finally, they touched. Lightly. Then she withdrew. Sam's entire body convulsed, as if she were having a seizure. Her back arched and her toes pointed, and she moaned with unbearable pleasure. "Does that feel good?" the Mistress asked, her mouth inches from Sam's. "Do you like that?"

"Yes," Sam managed to say. She realized now she was going to have to grovel. Not just beg, but grovel. Nothing else would satisfy this woman. Nothing.

"Do you want me to kiss you again?" the woman asked. "Like I did with that man in the film?"

Sam could take it no more. She began groveling like a baby. "Yes, please, please, please kiss me like that. Pleeeeeeaaase!"

"Don't stop," the Mistress said. "You're doing so good." Now there was a twinge of excitement in the Mistress's voice. *She* was getting aroused. This made Sam even more aroused, which, at this point, was almost more than she could bear.

Through her sobs, she cried, "Pleeeeease kiss me. Ohhhhhh, God. OHHHHHHHH! OHHHHHH! God, kiss me! Please! Pleeeeeeaaase!"

"Yeah, that's it," the Mistress said, sliding her hand back inside of Sam, and touching her again with her lips. This time she kissed Sam twice—two quick pecks—before withdrawing. "Ummmm!" the Mistress said, getting excited. "That feels good."

"Oh God, yeah!" Sam squealed, as both the pleasure and the need for release grew to heights she had never dreamed possible. The woman began kissing her some more. Quick, pecking kisses, like you might kiss someone good-bye if you were in a hurry. *Oh God, Ohhhhh,* Sam cried, her breath coming in deep stitches. The Mistress's lips felt *so* good. Like nothing she had ever felt before. She wanted to fall into those lips, be swallowed up by them, swim in them forever.

The Mistress picked up the pace, pecking her with kisses, like a bird pecking at a tree branch. With each peck, she made a small, sharp kissing noise. *Muah.* "Ohhhhh, God," Sam cried. She was building to a crescendo now, slowly but surely. Release was in sight. The kisses speeded up and began to get deeper. Mmmmwa. Mmmmmmwa. MuuuuuaaaaaaaaHHHH.

Sam could not believe how good those kisses felt. Even so, she knew they would not do the trick. They would not make her come; they would not end her agony. Only the kind of kiss she gave the man in the film would do that; a wet kiss with lips locked and tongues probing. Then and only then would the release come.

The pace quickened; the kisses grew longer and deeper.

Mmmmmmwwwwaaaaa.

Mmmmmmmmmmmmmmwwwwwwwwaaaaaaaaaaaa.

"Oh, God," the Mistress panted. "Oh, that feels so good!" Sam was convulsing with pleasure now, on the edge, over the edge, but not yet fully *there*; not yet at that place where the man in the film was — a place, a level of excitement she could not imagine even as she was beginning to taste it now, as it flowed from the Mistress's lips into her mouth and coursed through her body, like an invisible fire igniting her every nerve with ecstasy.

She desperately wished she could just throw her arms around Mistress X's neck and hold her there as they locked lips, but she didn't have the strength. "Please," she begged. "Keep…. Unhh…. Your lips…. Unhh…. On mine."

The Mistress began to finger Sam furiously now. As she did, she positioned her lips inches away from Sam's and spoke in a soft whisper. The sound of her voice was like a million feathers, each one tickling one of Sam's nerves. The Mistress said simply: "Not yet." She kept her lips where they were. She kept pecking. She kept speaking. Kept tickling, titillating, *torturing* Sam with her soft voice and delicate touch.

Sam was sobbing uncontrollably now, even as she continued groaning with pleasure. It was not unlike someone being tickled to death—laughter and tears mingling together in a grotesque form of torture. All Sam could do was plead: "Please.... Unhh.... Unhh.... Kiss me.... Unhh.... Unhh.... Unhhhhhh...."

"Oh you poor dear," Mistress X said. "You really do need me to kiss you, don't you?"

Sam could not even speak now. She could answer only in moans. But the Mistress was not moved. The talking, punctuated with kisses, some long some short, continued. Idle talk; meaningless words, just meant to prolong the agony. "Yes, dear.... Mmwa.... I know.... Mmwa.... Yeah.... Mmwa.... Yeah.... Mmwa...."

Torture. Pure and simple. And then, slowly, the kisses grew deeper, just like before. "Just be.... Mmwa.... A little bit.... Mmmmwa.... *Patient*.... Mmmmmmmmwa...." Sam moaned. "Unhh.... Unnnnnnhhhhhh...." The kisses grew deeper as Mistress X started to become excited again. "Soon," she cooed, "It will.... Mmmmmmmwwaa.... Be.... Mmmmmmmmmmwwaaa....Very.... Mmmmmmmmmwwwaaaa.... Soon."

Mistress X was kissing her passionately now, groaning with pleasure as their lips touched. Still withdrawing, yes, but not so much to cause Sam pain as to increase her own excitement. She was fully into it now and, Sam suspected, starting to feel the same excitement she felt. Moreover, she suspected that the Mistress's arousal was tied into her own. Mistress X could not come until *she* came. And there was no doubt now that Mistress X wanted to come. Soon.

More kisses followed, each one longer and deeper. Then, just as both women reached the edge, she withdrew again. She took several deep breaths and composed herself. Then she stared deep into Sam's eyes, all traces of pretense gone from her eyes. Sam saw only passion there. *Oh, God, this is it. This is really it.*

Very slowly, Mistress X started bringing her face down toward Sam's. *Oh, God, here it comes,* Sam thought, the image of the man in the film flashing before her, his body convulsing with ecstasy for minutes. And that had been after a *much* shorter lead-up than this one. She could not imagine what the Mistress had in store for her. Sam waited, quivering, as the glistening red lips inched closer and closer, stopping just inches from her own. "Are you ready?" Mistress X asked.

"Yes," Sam replied, bracing herself, and praying this was not another tease.

"Are you sure?" Mistress X asked.

"Yes," Sam replied.

"Well, okay then," Mistress X whispered, and touched her lips lightly against Sam's own. Sam half-expected her to withdraw again, but she didn't. Instead she pressed her lips down harder and began probing with her tongue. As she did, Sam could feel the front end of a tidal wave of pleasure so intense that it actually frightened her. It was not unlike the feeling one had when looking down at the top of a massive roller coaster incline and seeing that it stretched out just about forever. If in average orgasm was a kiddies ride at the neighborhood fare, then this was a zero gravity drop from two miles high.

The two women came together, their lips locked, their groans muffled by each other's mouths. Wave after wave of ecstasy swept through Sam's body. Each wave, however, was building to something bigger — one final climax that would be bigger than all of the others combined. And she was just about there. Mistress X withdrew her lips, allowing Sam the space for the scream that was about to happen.

"Are you ready," Mistress X asked, her voice quick and full of excitement. "Are you ready, are you ready, ha, ha, ha?" she repeated, as she fingered Sam furiously.

"Yeah, yeah, unnnnhhhhh.... Yeaaaahhhh," Sam gasped.

"Okay, okay," Mistress X said. "Here it goes. Are you sure you're ready?"

"Yes."

Suddenly Mistress X's hands were like two pistons inside of her, moving with impossible speed and precision. Sam was swept up in an impossibly huge orgasm. She screamed with ecstasy as her body convulsed. She felt like a damn had broken inside of her. Geysers of fluid shot out from between her legs, spraying the wall. She could not believe how far it traveled. This was simply not possible. She looked at Mistress X disbelievingly. Mistress X resumed the kissing. Deep, sweaty, passionate kissing full of tongue and smacking sounds.

The ecstasy was unfathomable, and yet, still building toward something even greater — a climax of unimaginable proportions. She felt it welling insider her, stirring, almost like a live organism trying to break free. It was as if a ball of sexual energy the size of the sun was about to explode out of her body. She screamed with ecstasy, bracing her body for the inconceivable wave that was about to sweep through it. She looked at Mistress X pleadingly, but the Mistress just smiled, even as she appeared about to come herself. Then Sam closed her eyes and let the wave hit her. A gusher of fluid exploded from her body like water from a firehose. It destroyed the TV set, shattered her dresser mirror, and put a dent in the wall. And it just kept coming and coming, drenching the entire room. As she came, Mistress X began to quiver and cry with pleasure. Her hands, however, were busy; one wrapped around Sam's neck, the other between her legs. Her own release would have to wait.

Then it was over. Sam lay there, gasping. A flood of relief swept through her. She felt limp. Beside her Mistress X was about to come. Quickly, Sam and Mistress X reversed positions. Sam began to slide her fingers between Mistress X's legs, but the gesture was rebuffed. The Mistress wanted to do it herself. *Knew how* to do it. To do it like no-one else could. She dug her own fingers deep inside of herself and lifted her legs up, spreading them wide, toes pointed toward the ceiling, butt and pussy stretched out and pointed squarely at the wall. Sam cradled her head in her arms and showered her face and neck with kisses.

She shrieked with pleasure, her body convulsing. Then she paused for a moment, her piston-like hands suddenly still, her chest heaving in and out. She fumbled for Sam's vibrator, grabbed it, and placed it at the base of her butthole. Slowly, she pushed it in. As she did she let out a deep, long groan. Then she dug her fingers back in between her legs and started fingering furiously. Within seconds she was coming with as much force as Sam had moments before. More, even. The geysers of liquid pounded the walls. Mistress X screamed with pleasure — a scream that literally shook the house. It went on for nearly a minute.

When it was all over, the two women just lay there, side by side, exhausted and limp. They looked at each other. Sam didn't know what to say. Their faces were only inches apart. Mistress X broke the silence. "I have to pee," she said.

"Me too," Sam replied. They were both lying with their feet flat on the bed and their legs folded at the knees. Mistress X spread her legs out just a bit, closed her eyes for a moment, then began to pee. Sam did the same. As Sam looked at Mistress X lying there, naked, peeing on the bed, she did not seem so invulnerable, so imposing anymore. In fact, she did not seem much different, then herself. She smiled. Mistress X smiled back. Their lips touched. Mistress X groaned and starting touching herself. Sam followed suit, sliding her own fingers between her legs. Within moments, both women were coming again. But this time, there were no geysers spraying the walls, no screams of anguished ecstasy. They just lie there together, kissing, rubbing their legs and feet up against each other's. "Oh, that feels so good," Sam said when it was over.

"Ummm…. I like to make people feel good," the Mistress replied, softly kissing Sam on the lips.

"Your lips feel so good," Sam said. "Like nothing I've ever felt."

And she meant it. Those lips felt *incredible*. Maybe because they were a woman's lips, not a man's? She didn't know. She didn't care. She just knew she loved them — so soft and red and glistening. One touch and she was transported. She just lay there, gazing sleepily at those lips. The more she gazed the sleepier she got. She felt like she was drowning in those lips, drowning in a sea of swirling, soft, glistening red. She closed her eyes and let herself fall.

Moments later, she awoke with a start. She felt around the bed. It was wet with pee. She was wet with sweat. But there was nothing on the walls. And no-one in her bed. It had been a dream — the part about Mistress X, anyway. The TV was crackling with static; the DVD was over. Mistress X was gone. She had never been there. Sam had fallen asleep watching her and dreamt about her.

She sighed deeply, running a hand down her thighs, into her crotch. She was sopping wet down there. *Christ, that was wild,* she thought. What a dream. She had never known she had these feelings toward women. Or maybe she had always known, but never admitted them. The dream seemed to penetrate new avenues of her consciousness — avenues she had never explored. It had wet her appetite. She wanted to explore now. And fortunately for her, she had the perfect subject, chained in the basement, with whom to experiment.

But that would be for another day. First, she had to clean up the mess.

Chapter 12

Burt Witter had been the sheriff of Swan Beak Bay for a decade. It was a small town with a small population. Not much happened there. And that's how Burt liked it. It's how he tried to keep it. And with considerable success, too. Their crime rate was the second lowest in New Jersey. Burt liked that. Shootouts were okay for the movies, but in real life they sucked. He didn't want them in his town. He didn't want crime in his town. He wanted his town to be known for its old fashioned Town Square, its two lovely parks, its idyllic, old fashioned movie theater, and its long, lovely Swan Beak Bay.

Except that now that Bay had become a dumping ground for dead bodies. Five in the last year. All of them burned alive. All of them victims of the WAR ON RELIGION KILLER, as he had dubbed himself. Somewhere out there a manic was killing preachers and dumping them in *his* bay. Where he was doing the killing, Burt didn't know. But he had chosen Swan Beak Bay to dump them when he was finished with them. He had to put an end to that, and soon. He had to catch this guy. But so far, there were no clues.

Burt was hoping to find one in the Xeroxed copy of an essay that lay before him on his desk. It was called "A Declaration of War" and it was, essentially, the WAR ON RELIGION killer's manifesto. The Daily Horn had agreed to print it several months ago. In exchange, the killer had promised to desist from any further killings for three months. So far he had kept his word. No new bodies in the Bay recently. But before the next one turned up, Burt wanted to get *something* on this guy. At least get on his trail. In the absence of anything better to go on, Burt found himself reading the manifesto for the second time in less than a week, hoping it might yield some clues.

It wasn't badly written. Not the rambling diatribe one might expect from a psychopathic madman. He actually made some good points. But certainly nothing original. Nothing that would have found a publisher under normal circumstances.

Burt reclined in his chair, propped his feet up on the desk, and read.

A Declaration of War

By the WAR ON RELIGION KILLER

The Seven Reasons Why Religion Must Be Destroyed

1. Religion opposes progress at every turn…. When Science discovered the earth is round, Religion said NO! When Science discovered the earth is not at the center of the universe, Religion said NO! When science discovered that life evolved over the course of long ages, Religion said NO! And in each instance Religion tried to block these advances, planting itself firmly in the path of progress, like a defensive tackle trying to thwart an onrushing halfback. It tried to block these advances with arguments, with intimidation, with persecution, with violence and sometimes even torture.

With time, however, the truth won out and these advances in knowledge became accepted as fact by the general public. And what was the Church's response to these defeats? It would simply reinterpret the bible to fit the new facts. Then it would re-group and prepare to oppose the next advance. And when that one became accepted as fact, they would reinterpret their Scriptures accordingly. At every turn they would oppose new facts, then, when those facts won out, they would declare it was what the bible taught all along! Given these facts, it should be obvious that religion is opposed to progress, and anything that stands opposed to progress ought to be destroyed.

2. Religious understanding of sin is opposed to everything we know in other fields, *as well as that which we know from experience. It does not take into account what we know as fact about cause and effect, or brain chemistry, or social factors. Instead it dumps all of the burden of sin at the door of an invisible, mysterious, spiritual force called free will, for which there is no evidence whatsoever, and plenty of evidence against. Yes, we can make choices, but those choices are always circumscribed by the confines of our own natures.*

Let me illustrate. I once had a dog – Lillian. Lillian was difficult, annoying, and sometimes, downright weird, but she was never not a dog. Us, too. We never do anything that doesn't spring from the wide range of human potential developed through a complex interplay of nature and nurture. We have built-in limits which can be worsened (and improved) depending on what we're taught and given to work with, and can even turn horrifying through damaging experiences. True, sometimes damage and misdirection come from our own choices, but these take root in that same human fashion: no matter what, still all human, all understandable, all the time, no exceptions — at least so it should be to a loving creator who set us on this path. But the Bible doesn't reflect this. It reads black and white only. It betrays and understanding of human nature in which evil is an occupying force — and an invited one, at that — more than something built — in that we struggle with.[i]

As long as religion continues to retain a primitive concept of sin that disregards all knowledge in the fields of psychology, sociology, biology, neurology, physics, and every other discipline, it will continue to be a force for evil rather than for good. As such, it ought to be destroyed.

3. Religion can never give us a sound basis for opposing immoral conduct performed in the name of God, since it places God's commands above and even beyond our moral intuitions, as when Abraham consented to murder his own child because God said so. As long as we believe this, then we also believe, at least to some degree, that God can command anything and it can be right; hence, when someone flies planes into a tower to kill the infidels, Christians cannot honestly disagree with them in principle; only in the particulars, namely, to say that they are killing in the name of the wrong God — Allah rather than Jehovah. But as for slaughtering man for God's sake; well, how can we oppose it when Scripture, in many instances, clearly sanctions, encourages, and commands it?

4. Religion brings only division, even among its own adherents. If God has spoken to us through His prophets, then you would expect the message to be clear, concise, and unambiguous. You would expect agreement among all who have investigated the content of this message. And yet we find the reverse is true. Division is rife; God's people are torn in a thousand different directions by schisms. Everywhere you turn a different message prevails. The Church is rent into dozens of denominations, and schisms exist even within those denominations. Moreover, the differences relate not just too abstract theological minutia, but to the most basic tenets of Faith. Christians cannot even agree on answers to the following questions:

1. What is God?

This most basic of questions yields a variety of competing answers from the esteemed Priesthood of the Christian Religious System. He is One, some say. He is three, say others. He is three in One. He is One in three. He is Three, with one of the three eternally proceeding from another of the three. It seems that no-one can agree on which of the three proceeds from who, and when in time, if ever, the proceeding started. Nor can they agree on the nature of the relationship between the three, or of the difference in stature between them, or if any such difference exists. They cannot even agree on the importance of the doctrine in question; some say it is a mere semantic quibble; others insist that a person's very soul is at stake.

2. What is God like?

Again, we are confronted with the most fundamental of questions. Surely if God has spoken, He would have answered it in the most plain and decisive way possible, such that any disagreement on the matter would be all but impossible. And yet we find that the reverse is true; there is enormous disagreement about what God is like. Some depict Him as jovial Santa Claus in the sky, always eager to forgive, generous, kind, and overflowing with compassion for every creature under heaven, from the vilest criminal to the sparrow flitting through the skies.

Others depict Him as a cold, distant, petty tyrant, filled to the brim with unspeakable rage, and holding it in abeyance only *for the sake of Christ — and no-one else — and that only until Judgment Day, when He will unleash it in full measure on almost all of the hapless, helpless, hopeless creatures on the earth — creatures He created as vessels of wrath to be tormented forever in hell for the very sins He created them to commit. The two visions of God could not be farther apart, and yet they both thrive in churches across the world that supposedly worship the SAME God.*

3. What did God's Son Accomplish on the Cross?

Another fundamental question; another plurality of answers.

Christ offered Himself as a ransom to God (Ransom Theory)

Christ offered Himself as a ransom to Satan (Ransom Theory)

Christ undid what Adam did (Recapitulation Theory)

Christ appeased God's offended honor (Satisfaction Theory)

Christ died to influence mankind toward moral improvement (Moral Influence Theory)

Christ died to guarantee victory to His followers (Guaranty Theory)

Christ died to condemn sin by a perfect demonstration of righteousness (Vicarious Repentance)

Christ died as an accident (Accident Theory)

Christ died as a martyr (Martyr Theory)

The who, the what, the where, the how…. The most basic, fundamental questions, which God has supposedly answered in Scripture, continue to be a source of contention, division, and strife. Has God spoken? If He has, then He has done so with a profound lack of clarity.

4. For Whom Did He Accomplish What He Accomplished?

Again, a very basic question. If God has spoken, we should expect a clear answer from Scripture and unanimity of opinion from those who study those Scriptures. But once again, on a very basic question, we find ourselves confronted with a stupefying profusion of answers. A sampling:

> *He died for ALL, that ALL might be saved*
> *He died for ALL, that ALL might be JUSTIFIED, and those who ACCEPT this justification might be saved*
> *He died for ALL that SOME might be justified and saved*
> *He died for SOME that SOME might be justified and saved*

5. Why did Christ Die on the Cross?

Again, different answers abound. Some say He died out of a profound love for sinners; others say He died for the Father's sake alone; still others say He died for "the joy that was set before Him" (Heb 12:2; Jn. 17:5)

6. By What Means Do We Attain the Benefits of What Christ Accomplished on the Cross? Or, to put it another way: How are we saved?

Finally, we get to the most crucial question of all: How Are We Saved? Surely with regard to this question, which bears directly on the eternal destiny of all, God has spoken with ringing clarity and utmost simplicity, such that all who have heard His voice agree on exactly what He has said. Well, not really. Once again, the answers, as the demoniac said, are "legion."

By Baptism: John 3:5: "Jesus answered, 'I tell you the

truth, no one can enter the kingdom of God unless he is born of water and the Spirit.'"

By Grace & Faith, not Works: Ephesians 2:8,9: "For by grace are ye saved through faith…not of works."

By Faith & Works: James 2:17: "Even so faith, if it hath not works, is dead, being alone."

By Keeping the Law: Matthew 19:17: "…if thou wilt enter unto life, keep the commandments."

By Belief in Christ: John 3:16: "…whosoever believeth in him should not perish, but have everlasting life."

By Belief and Baptism: Mark 16:16: "He that believeth and is baptized shall be saved; but he that believeth not shall be damned."

By Words: Matthew 12:37: "For by thy words thou shalt be justified, and by thy words thou shalt be condemned."

By Calling on the Lord: Acts 2:21: "whoever calls upon the name of the Lord shall be saved."

Not Works but by Grace & Baptism: Titus 3:5: "Not by works…but according to his mercy… by the washing of regeneration." (Note: some denominations will say the washing refers to Christ's blood and sacrifice.)

By Not Judging Others*: Matthew 7:1: "Do not judge, or you will be judged. For in the same way you judge others, you will be judged."*

By Loving Others*: Luke 7:47: "Wherefore I say unto thee, Her* *sins, which are many, are forgiven, for she loved much....*"

By the Eucharist: *John 6:56: "He who eats my flesh and drinks my blood abides in me."*

By Prayer and Anointing: *James 5:14-15: Is anyone among you sick? Let them call the elders of the church to pray over them and anoint them with oil in the name of the Lord. And the prayer offered in faith will make the sick person well; the Lord will raise them up. If they have sinned, they will be forgiven. Therefore confess your sins to each other so that you may be healed.*

According to Proverbs 16:4: God made the "wicked" for "the day of evil" (i.e. judgment & damnation). Of course, this makes no sense in light of passages that confirm or suggest that Jesus died for a small number of the elect; or that suggest all will be saved: John 1:29, 4:42, 1 Corinthians 15:29, Hebrews 2:9, 1 John 4:14.

Salvation Available to the Chosen Few: Matthew 7:14, 22:14, Luke 12:32, 13:24, John 6:37,65,15:16,19, Romans 8:29, 9:11-23, Ephesians 1:4.

Salvation Available to Those Who Desire it: Matthew 7:7-8, 11:28, John 3:16, 5:40, 7:37, Acts 2:21, Revelation 3:20.
ii

Now, at this point one might say: Okay, you have a point. There is no consensus with regard to many points of the faith. But all Christians agree on Love, and that is the most important thing of all.

Well, not really. Not all Christians agree that love is the most important thing of all; many would say Faith is more important, that it precedes genuine love, and that it alone is the guarantor of salvation. But granting the proposition for a moment, there is any more consensus with regard to how we are to love than there is with regard to the other issues. Different Christians have widely different ideas of what it means, in God's eyes, to love our neighbor. Depending on who you believe, we love by:

> *Sharing the gospel (Calvinist love)*
> *Doing good deeds and renouncing material comforts (Mother Teresa love)*
> *Showing others how to attain MORE material comforts (Prosperity Gospel, Joel Osteen love)*
> *Doing good deeds and sharing the gospel (Billy Graham love)*
> *Hurling Bible-based insults at mourners at funerals (Fred Phelps love)*

And so the conclusion is this: Christians can't agree on anything. Not even on the most fundamental issues. They preach to US, they try to convert us to THEIR world view, and yet, they cannot even agree with each other about matters of the absolute, utmost simplicity. Obey their God, they say, but they don't agree on Who He is, what He's like, what He's accomplished, or how to please Him. They can't even agree on how to love!

5. Religion Is Inherently Dishonest

The true objective of religion is not discovery; it is conversion. It is not to probe for truth; it is to reinforce one's existing ideas of truth. Honest inquiry is frowned upon. How do members of evangelical churches decide what to read? They ask their pastor, and their pastor steers them toward books that promote "sound doctrine"? This is a fact; no honest person can dispute this. As soon as you believe your eternal soul depends on what you believe, you have a vested interest in reading only those materials that will promote the ideas you believe to be beneficial to the welfare of your soul. Hence, honest inquiry is excluded; honest discourse is impossible. The religious person cannot be reasoned with. Period.

6. Religion Employs a Contradictory, Nonsensical Conceptual Framework

Conceptually speaking, religious people live in a parallel universe. They say God made us for Himself, and yet, we are capable of defeating His purpose for our life by misusing our "free will." Well, if we were MADE FOR GOD, if we are all born with God-shaped holes that only God can fill, as one theologian put it, then what we truly want would, in the end, have to be precisely what God wants for us; indeed, what we want would have to be God Himself. And yet the Christian Religious System, due to its belief in eternal torment, is forced to deny this basic fact. And that is not logical. It is not reasonable. And one cannot believe it, or defend it, from within a rational conceptual framework. Those Christians who defend this position are usually referred to as Arminians.

Then you have the Calvinists. At least they make no pretense about God loving us. According to them, God loves only a select few; the rest are "vessels of wrath" who were made for the purpose of suffering eternal destruction in hell. When pressed as to how a Father could do this to His children, they say "God is not our Father; He is only our Creator." How can one make sense of this? They seek to absolve God of the lesser responsibility by appealing to the GREATER one! Again, the logic here is tortured and nonsensical — part of a conceptual framework that no person could accept who is not a part of that system.

Christians are just as confused with regard to the subject of free will. Why are we all born as sinners? Because of Adam's sin in the garden. He misused his free will. But ask them: How could God be justified in ascribing one man's sin to all men? And they will say: Because any man, in Adam's shoes, would have done the same. Well, where's the freedom in that? If we all would have done the same, then obviously, there's a constraint present — a constraint which is rooted in our natures. You can't have it both ways. Either we're all free to act DIFFERENTLY under like conditions, and God did not have the right to ascribe Adam's sin to everyone, or we are not free, allowing God to know with certainty how all men would respond to the same given circumstance. But to both affirm and deny these two possibilities at the same time is illogical, and, once again, demonstrates a commitment to a conceptual framework that is alien to reason, experience, and science.

Examples of this incoherent conceptual framework can be multiplied, but I think I have made my point.

7. Religion is Child Abuse

From an early age, children reared in mainline evangelical churches are presented with two choices: Repent and accept Jesus Christ as your personal Savior or burn in hell forever. Is this child abuse? I say it is. Moreover, I say it is easy to prove. Simply gauge the reaction of any mainline evangelical pastor to the following scenario: A child is raised in an isolated, self-contained community of religious fanatics somewhere in the hills of Appalachia. He is taught to believe the community's leader, Herbert G. Tackleberry, is God's chosen prophet. Mr. Tackleberry teaches substantially the same things as evangelical

Christians, namely, the importance of accepting Christ, reading the bible, prayer, and proper Christian conduct. The only difference is that he also teaches that HE is best suited, among all modern-day preachers and teachers, to interpret what that actually means. And so every child's best bet to escape hell is strict adherence to the DIVINELY INSPIRED PRINCIPLES HE LAYS OUT.

Now, dear reader, I ask you: Would not most every evangelical preacher in the world consider this a form of child abuse? But how is this any different than the situation in his own church? Does HE not hold a similar station? Does HE not preside over essentially the same office? Consider: there are thousands of preachers with vastly opposing messages, yet each one holds sway over their OWN congregation as the ONE – or, to be generous, as a representative of the ONE sect – that is MOST CLOSELY ALIGNED WITH THE TRUTH that will SAVE THE SOULS OF THEIR FLOCK FROM HELL.

But let's not use such an extreme example. Forget about the lone preacher with his captive flock in the remote hills out there in the middle of nowhere. Let's employ a more mundane example – the Jehovah Witness's. Most evangelical pastors would say that this church is an example of a "cult" and would decry their tactics as dishonest and coercive. In their more candid moments, they might even suggest that children reared in this environment, and forced to adopt this mindset, are the victims of abuse.

But what exactly is the difference between the Jehovah's and a mainline Protestant? Well, there's hardly a charge the mainliner could level at the JW that does not also apply to his own church. The JW, they say, has "hidden doctrines" that the elders do not reveal to new converts. Fine. So does mainline Protestantism. Rarely are new converts confronted with the *doctrine of predestination; indeed, some Christians never become acquainted with it, and others do, but have a wrong understanding.*

What else? The JW elders, the mainliner will insist, insulate their flock from opposing points of view. Mainline pastors do the same thing, discouraging their flock from reading anything that smacks of "unsound" doctrine, or from consorting with "infidels," for "bad company corrupts good morals."

What else? The JWs, the mainliner will charge, has a bizarre system of bible interpretation. If by that they mean that the JW force a certain meaning into a text where it is not apparent to anyone else, then the mainliners — and every sect of Christianity — is also guilty.

What else? Perhaps the JWs use more coercive methods to enforce obedience? Really? The JWs believe in the annihilation of the wicked. The mainliners teach that the wicked will be tortured forever in hell. And they teach it to children from a very young age. What could be more coercive than that? To review:

Each has "hidden doctrines"
Each has bizarre "hermeneutics"
Each discourages reading books that promote "unsound" doctrine
Each encourages insulating the person from society
Each employs the doctrine of eternal banishment as a means of enforcing obedience.

But even if one could point to more substantial differences than the ones I've named, so what? The differences seem almost trivial when compared with the similarities! And it is the features both share, even more than those they do not, that enforce the obedience of their members!

Bottom line: If cults are committing child abuse, then so are mainline Christians. And Catholics. And Anglicans. And Eastern Orthodox. And Muslims. And Jews. And everyone else who teaches that if you follow their rules of Faith and Conduct you will go to heaven, but depart from those ways and you will burn forever.

Why Religion Must Be Opposed

This last subject — that of child abuse — segues nicely into why religion must be opposed, and opposed by FORCE. Consider: Most children in the world today grow up under some form of religious indoctrination that MOST people of MOST other denominations would classify as CHILD ABUSE.

Let me repeat that. Most children in the world today grow up under some form of religious indoctrination that MOST people of MOST other denominations would classify as CHILD ABUSE. And the ONLY answer to this problem that most religious people have is to declare that the other denominations simply HAVE THE WRONG GOD!

Be that as it may, you object: the answer is surely not violence! Rest assured, I once shared your point of view. But the more I thought about it, the more I realized there is no other viable option. Lest you say, there MUST be a better way to oppose Religion than by violence, let us review the available options, and see what results they are likely to yield.

Options 1: Dialogue

It will not work for several reasons. First, the religious among us have no interest in dialogue; remember the fifth point:

Religion is Inherently Dishonest. The true objective of religion is not discovery; it is conversion. It is not to probe for truth; it is to reinforce one's existing ideas of truth. Honest inquiry is frowned upon. This virtually assures that dialogue will fail to make any inroads. But all of the other reasons on my list also show why dialogue will not work. To dialogue is to work toward progress. This is to assume we all *want* progress, or can agree on a definition of the word. But remember my first point: Religion opposes progress. What we call progress they call sacrilege. You cannot argue anyone out of their religious beliefs, for they did not come by them via reason in the first place. It has been well said that "Contesting religion is like engaging in a boxing match with jelly: it is a shifting, unclear, amorphous target, which every blow dispatches to a new shape."

Option 2: Ignore it

This will not work. Ignore some things — like your teeth or your spouse — and they will go away. Religion is not one of those things. Moreover, we couldn't ignore it if we wanted to. How do you ignore so-called "radical" Islam, which kills as many people as it can on a daily basis in the name of its God? And what about the millions of children that we alluded to previously? Should we simply ignore them? We cannot ignore them, nor can we reason with their captors. This leaves one — and only one — viable option.

A DECLARATION OF WAR

The United States has declared war on "radical" Islam. I say "radical" Islam is a natural by-product of ISLAM. Moreover, Islam is a natural by-product of Religion, which has always and everywhere behaved in much the same way. Hence, rather than mince words, and ignore reality, I declare war not on "RADICAL" Islam; nor on "liberal" Islam, nor on Christianity, nor on Judaism, or Hinduism, or any of these particular denominations, for that would be an exercise in semantics, a pointless splitting of hairs. Instead I declare war on the Source of the evil in question: RELIGION! Your religion and my religion. EVERY religion. I declare war in the name of:

Everyone who ever lost a loved one at the hands of a suicide bomber doing "God's work."

Every child who has ever died waiting for medical care while his parents were waiting for God to cure him.

Every child abused by Catholic priests.

Every sick person swindled out their life savings by faith healing charlatans.

Every child ever subjected to genital mutilation due to their parents' religious beliefs.

Every person who ever suffered psychological damage due to the fear of eternal damnation.

Every woman who ever felt compelled to "subject" herself to an abusive husband because "God" wanted her to do so.

Every homosexual who had to live with the contempt of their family due to that family's religious beliefs.

Every person who must confess or deny a particular creed to avoid being imprisoned or killed.

Every person who ever died at the hands of a cult leader.

It is for all of these, and untold others, that I declare war. And what's more, I encourage you to join me. If you believe, as I do, and as MOST PREACHERS DO, that religious indoctrination is a form of child abuse, then JOIN ME. If you believe, as I do, that at this very moment the innocent are suffering at the hands of these preachers and teachers, then JOIN ME. If you believe, as I do, that a war cannot be waged against a powerful, intransigent enemy with words and dialogue alone, then JOIN ME. Join me in taking action. Real action.

Burt put the paper back down on his desk, took his glasses off, and rubbed his eyes. There wasn't much there he could use. The Feds had already drawn up a profile of this guy, much of it based on the essay: White Male, mid-forties to early-fifties, probably a former preacher, possibly defrocked. Probably married with children.

That was about it. Burt had hoped that by reading the essay something else might jump out at him—something the others had missed—but nothing had. His profile was the same as their profile. He just hoped it was the right profile. He hoped they were looking in the right places. Because if they were, they should have had him by now. A discontented, defrocked wacko preacher should not have been this hard to find. But he was. Maybe the Feds were missing something. Something that maybe he could find.

Chapter 13

Terrence heard talking and two sets of footsteps. "The man" was back. For the past week it had just been himself and "the woman." Now the guy was back. He didn't like that. He was hoping — praying, really — that the guy would never come back. He had no reason to believe it, but he hoped it nonetheless.

Why he didn't stay with the woman, he didn't know. He could only assume he had some other commitments — perhaps a whole other life — somewhere else. At any rate, the arrangement was clear: the two of them maintained this house as a torture chamber for their victims, she lived there, and he popped in and out at regular intervals. At least that's how it seemed. Now he was back. For how long, Terrence did not know. He hoped not long.

He watched with dread as the door opened. The woman — Samantha — hung back in the doorway as the man — Austin — strolled right in, unafraid of being accosted or overpowered. And with good reason. It's not likely he could overpower that man. Clad in black, with his greaser look, the man radiated strength. Strength and fearlessness. It was a fearlessness born of hatred. That

117

hatred, more than anything, was what terrified Terrence.

"How are we doing?" Austin asked, sitting right next to Terrence on the bench. It almost seemed to Terrence as if he wanted him to make a move. As if he was inviting it.

"I'm very, very warm," Terrence replied honestly. Each day the heat got turned up a little more. They were slowly roasting him to death. His clothes were drenched in sweat; he had only changed twice in the two weeks he had been there. On each occasion the woman opened the door, tossed him some clothes, and left.

"Well, I figured you were," Austin said, staring Terrence right in the face with his dark, unblinking eyes. "What else?"

"Pardon me?" He didn't understand what Austin was asking.

Austin said, "Have you learned anything from this experience?"

Terrence did not know how to respond. The question had been posed with the affectation of a stern schoolmaster chiding a rebellious student. A number of options leapt into his mind. He could try to pretend he had "learned his lesson," he could throw himself at the mercy of the court, he could try to engage the man in discussion, or he could simply answer the question. He decided to simply say, "I don't know."

"That's a good answer," Austin replied.

"Hey, hon," Sam said from the doorway, "I'm going upstairs."

"Okay," Austin said, "I'll be up in a bit." With that, she turned and walked away. "So," Austin said, turning his attention back to Terrence. "Do you know why you're here?"

"Yes, I think I do," Terrence said. Like most people —

especially preachers — in the Tri-State area, he had read Austin's Manifesto. He knew that the man believed he was doing the world a service. He knew that he believed there was no other means by which it could be accomplished. He was a reluctant Avenger whose hand had been forced by an Evil Religious System.

Austin just stared at him for a moment, reading him with his eyes. Then he said, "You think I'm just some wacko psychopath, don't you?"

Again, Terrence's head filled with possible responses. Try to engage him in conversation? Pretend to understand him? Try to befriend him? Or just tell the truth. He weighed all of those options within a second's time, and decided on the last, believing he could not fool this man anyway. "I think that's probably fairly accurate," he said.

Austin simply nodded. His face betrayed no emotion as he spoke again. "I remember a conversation I had with the pastor of a Baptist Church I used to attend." He spoke in a conversational tone, without condescension or malice, as if speaking to a friend. This was a hopeful sign — the first one he had received from the man, the first hint he had given that maybe, just maybe, he could be reasoned with. "At the time," Austin continued, "an evangelical Christian had made news for killing an abortion doctor." The man's tone was calm and measured; he wanted to make a point, and he wanted Terrence to *get* it.

"I asked him what he thought about it," he continued. "Bear in mind, now, this guy was no fanatic. He was your average, everyday, run-of-the-mill pastor. And he looked at me and he said, 'I think he's a Godly man. I don't know that I would have handled it that way, but I think he did what he felt was right.'" Austin hesitated, and Terrence thought he knew where this was going.

"Let me ask you something, Pastor," Austin said, his voice solemn and strong. "Do you think what he did was right?"

Terrence realized instantly that Austin had put him squarely behind the eight ball. An answer of YES was an admission that killing in a just, but undeclared, unofficial war, was justified. An answer of NO was tantamount to saying that Christians ought to protest "murder," but not take any other steps to stop it. "I don't know," Terrence said, once again electing to simply tell the truth.

"Well, I do," Austin said firmly. "Sometimes we have to declare war not on a country, or a tribe, or a political entity; sometimes we have to declare war on an idea. And when we do that we have to actually back it up. We have to *do* something. We have to take action. *This* is the action I am taking. Yes, I know the people I've killed have families. So did the man that GUY killed. So does every soldier killed in war. So did the soldiers killed in Iraq when *God* told George Bush to go to war. Bereaved family members are a part of war. You can't stop that."

Austin paused, waiting for a response. Terrence thought for a moment, then said, "Are you willing to die for your war?"

"Yes," Austin answered without hesitation.

"Why?" Terrence replied. He was not trying to engage his captor in conversation; he was genuinely curious. He wanted to know why Austin was willing to die for this cause.

"Because I believe in it," Austin said. Again, he spoke without sarcasm, without contempt. He spoke as one would to a colleague. Terrence thought that was strange. But it also told him that this man was not motivated simply by hate; he really *did* believe he had to do these things.

"Yes, I know," Terrence said. "But what I mean is.... If there's no God, then the only real thing you have to live for is your own life, your own happiness, right here, right now, in this lifetime. So why die for a cause? Even if your war is successful, you will not live to see the benefits."

A trace of doubt crept into Austin's face. For the first time, he seemed unsure. It seemed to Terrence that he did not have an answer to this question. Austin simply stood up and walked over to the door. The two men stared at each other for a moment, silently. "Good night," Austin said, then left.

Terrence watched him leave. There was doubt there, he could tell.

But no mercy.

****

Sam was in the living room watching TV when Austin came back up from the basement. He came over to the couch and sat next to her, sliding an arm around her shoulder and neck. His touch felt good. She missed him when he was gone, which was almost always; she missed his touch, his voice, his presence. She wished he could stay for more than a day or so at a time. She wished she could be more than his sister and his mistress and his best friend.

He began nibbled her neck. She took his chin in her hand, holding it between her thumb and forefinger, and kissed him on the lips. He returned the favor. "How about we continue this in the bedroom?" Austin suggested.

"Sounds good to me," Sam said, and together they went up the stairs, his hand around her waist.

As they entered the room, Sam went straight for her dresser. She knew the drill by now. She opened the top draw, took out a blonde wig, and put it on. She had to be someone else now. Who that would be she did not know yet. He would pick out a name. He would call her by that name, she would answer to it, and that's who she would be for the evening. It was his way of denying, in his own mind, the fact that he was making love to his sister. For him it was a source a shame.

Not for her, though. For her, it was the opposite. Her parents had taught her sex was evil, men were evil, they only wanted one thing. Only sex with her brother was "pure," only he could be trusted. And she grew up believing it. In the arms of any other man, she had always felt dirty. Sinful. Evil. Only in Austin's arms did she feel okay. She slipped into those arms now, as the two slid into bed. They undressed each other slowly, then lay there, on their sides, faces inches apart, and pecked at each other's lips with their own.

Slowly their kisses grew deeper, their tongues probing each other's mouths. "Oh, Gina," Austin sighed.

Gina. That was who she was tonight. Whatever. Austin draped a leg over her side, then hoisted himself over her, and then went inside her. They kissed passionately as he thrust his hips slowly in and out. About a minute later he came. She only pretended to. When they were finished, Austin slid off of her, and they just lay there, wrapped in each other's arms, staring into each other's eyes.

She could see so much in his eyes. So much of him, of herself, of the world, of her past, of his past, of their past. And she knew he saw the same thing in hers. In a way, they were the same person—two sides of the same coin. And when they came together, they felt whole. No one else could do that for them. But more and more she began to realize their union was much more emotional than sexual. And after her encounter with Mistress X—even though just a dream—she realized how deprived she had been in that department for all these years. And how much exploring she needed to do. How many oats she needed to sow.

Looking deep into Austin's eyes, she smiled a tender, almost motherly smile. Poor thing. It was so obvious why he hated religion so much. He hated it because he had never escaped it.

And never could.

Chapter 14

For the second time in a week, Nick strolled through the doors of the River View Mental Hospital, past the reception desk, up the elevator, down the halls, and toward room 202. A part of him—a big part—wanted to simply turn back around, and run. Just forget it. Leave River View and Adam Becker and Martin Monroe in the rearview mirror and never give it another thought.

But that would be impossible. He'd done nothing but think about it for the past week. For years he had been doing battle with evil, but never had he confronted it for *real*. Not until now. Now he had confronted it twice in two weeks—first at the house on Blackwood Clemington Road, and once here at River View. And it scared him. Scared him shitless. It was so raw and so angry and so *real*.

He had told Adam. He had pulled no punches. He had told him flat out: *your patient is possessed by a demon*. Adam, however, had not been convinced. He didn't blame him. He wouldn't have believed *himself* just a few short weeks ago. But now he *had* to believe. He had seen it, felt it, touched it, and even smelled it. Death personified. Evil with a human face. Or residing in a man with one, anyway. Although Adam still did not believe Martin was possessed, he liked the idea of Nick seeing him again. He still thought it could have a positive effect. And so here he was again.

The moment he entered Martin's room, he knew it was not Martin. It was that…Thing, sitting up in bed, staring at him with those dead eyes.

"Hello," he said, smiling malevolently. "Did you miss me?" Nick sat down by the side of the bed, as he had done the last time. Just like the last time, a horrible, fetid odor filled his nostrils. It was like the stench of a dead body — only worse. It was the stench of a dead soul. A *long* dead soul. And now this dead soul — this vile, wretched, evil worm of a creature — had infested the body of Martin Monroe, like a germ.

"I see you have brought a friend," the Thing said, looking down at Nick's lap, where a copy of the King James Bible rested.

"Does it bother you?" Nick asked.

"Not at all," the Thing said. "I actually find it quite amusing."

"Really?"

"Yes, really."

"What is it that amuses you?"

"Do you really think that you can drive me away by reciting a few passages from that silly little book of yours?"

"Maybe," Nick said. "I believe God can drive you out any time He wishes."

"His power was never in doubt," the Thing said. "It's His love that I question. Don't you?"

"No," Nick replied firmly.

"Really?" the Thing sneered. "How noble of you. You don't doubt when He lets millions of children starve to death? You don't doubt when He drowns thousands in a tsunami? You don't doubt when He levels whole cities with earthquakes, floods, or tornadoes? You don't doubt when He directs a chimpanzee to eat a woman's face off, leaving her unable to see, eat, or speak? You don't doubt when He directs a rapist to abduct a nine-year-old girl and bury her alive? You don't doubt when He directs soldiers to cut off children's limbs so they can't grow up to oppose them? You don't doubt when He gives a small child cancer, and lets it eat her away slowly, inch by inch, piece by piece, while her parents watch helplessly? None of these things cause you to doubt?"

Nick did not respond; he was not there to debate.

"Very well, then," the Thing said. "You wish to play it cool. I understand. Perhaps if we make it a little more...personal."

Nick did not like the sound of that. He braced himself.

"What about those long nights...as a child, when you couldn't sleep because you thought you had committed an unforgivable sin, and you prayed to God, begged Him in fact, to let you fall asleep? Did He? No, He didn't, did He? Did that cause you to doubt?

"And what about when your mother was wasting away from throat cancer? And you begged God to restore her health, and He didn't? Did that make you doubt?

"And what about when you were a teenager, plagued by all those 'ungodly' desires, and you begged God to take them away, and help you stop touching yourself so that you wouldn't burn in hell? Did He? No, He didn't, did He? Did *that* make you doubt?"

For the first time since being in this Thing's presence,

Nick felt more angry than afraid. Anger rose through his voice as he answered the Thing back. "Yes, I doubted," he growled, leaning forward in his chair, his lips curled into a sneer. "I doubted on each and one of those occasions. I didn't know why God didn't answer my prayers, and I still don't. Maybe I never will. But I know this: the suffering I endured as a child helped me to help a lot of children going through the same things. The pain of losing my mother helped me minister to many people as they coped with terminal illness in their own family. And the sexual temptations I wrestled with as a teenager has helped me minister to young adults as they experience the same conflicts. So, in answer to your question: Yes, I doubted. But I still believed. I believed then and I believe now."

"Ah, you must belong to the Soul-Making school of theodicy. God allows suffering that good may come from it; He uses it to mold our characters. Is that it? Is that what you believe?"

"I think God has a reason for everything He does," Nick answered.

"So, tell me, please: What good came to the six million Jews who were tortured to death in Nazi concentration camps? Were they being fitted for heaven? What about the ones that died cursing God? Or the babies thrown alive into the ovens? Was God molding their characters? And let's not forget, Pastor, the six million people killed were Jews. *Jews.* That means they had never accepted Jesus Christ as their Savior, so according to your theology, they are all in hell right now anyway, and will be there forever. So again, I ask you: What good came of all their suffering? How can you even make such a claim with a straight face?"

"I don't pretend to know all of God's mysteries, but I know one thing: He works *all* things together for the good of those that love Him. And I know another thing: Your end is foretold. Your fate is sealed. You are a defeated foe, and you will be cast into the lake of fire forever and ever. Revelations 20:10."

The Thing's lips curled into a snarl. He was angry now. Nick felt nervous, recalling what had happened the last time the Thing had become angry. But this time there was no blast of fetid air from its mouth—only words. "Then I suppose I will be keeping your son Raymond company, will I not?" it sneered. "For you do know that the lake of fire is reserved for fornicators and adulterers and the covetous and drunkards...." It leaned forward as it spoke, its voice rising with each word. "...and revilers and swindlers and effeminate and *homosexuals!*"

He shouted the last word into Nick's face, blasting him with his putrid breath. Then he smiled and fell back into his pillow. "Do you know why Martin asked for you?"

"No," Nick replied, his blood boiling.

"It's because you and him share something in common."

"What?"

"Me. I have been inside of you almost as long as I've been inside of him."

"What!" Nick said, startled by the revelation. "What do you mean?"

The Thing just smiled. "I will tell you in your dreams," he said grinning, and then drifted off to sleep.

Chapter 15

Sam had this weird feeling she was dreaming. Dreaming or remembering. She wasn't sure which. And she wasn't sure enough it was a dream to wake up. But it seemed like a dream because in her dreams her father had fangs and hands like claws, and in real life he did not.

She was a child again. She and Austin and their father were in her bedroom. She was seven and he was nine. Their father sat them down together on the bed, next to each other, and sat across from them. "I want to have a talk with you two," he said, smiling gently. It was night time and they were in their pajamas. Their feet hung over the edge of the bed as he spoke—four tiny children's feet poking through the thin cotton legs of their little pajamas.

"What do you want to talk about, Daddy?" Sam asked.

"Well," he said, his claw-hands folded across his lap. "You two are getting older now, and there are certain things you are going to have to learn."

"What kind of things, Daddy?" Sam asked curiously. Her father smiled. Tiny strands of spittle hung down from his fangs.

"Well...." he said. "Grown-up things."

"You mean like making money and stuff?" Austin asked.

Her dad smiled. "Well, that one can wait a while," he said. "What I have in mind for today is something a little bit different." He paused, rubbing his chin with his claw-hand. "Did you kids ever hear the expression *the birds and the bees*?"

"I've heard of that," Austin replied.

"I haven't," Sam said. "What does it mean?"

"It's another way of saying *sex*."

"I've heard of that, too," Austin said. "But I don't know what it is."

"Me neither," said Sam.

"Of course you don't," her dad said. "How could you unless someone teaches you? That's what I'm going to do today."

"Okay," they chimed in unison.

Her dad followed this with a rather detailed, and, to her seven-year-old mind, disgusting anatomy lesson. *That's* how people get pregnant? Yuuuuck!

Then things got more...hands on. He instructed the two of them to disrobe. It seemed an odd request, but they obeyed, and proceeded to slip out of their pajamas. Then they just stood there, naked, staring at each other with considerable discomfort, and awaiting further instruction.

It was at that point that Sam became sure she was dreaming. She closed her eyes, shook her head, and woke up. There she was, in her bed again. Alone. Austin had left again. He had gone back to his other life. It was just her and Terrence now. The preacher. The dirty, hypocritical, no-good, pervert preacher. She was really going to have some fun with him.

Chapter 16

As Cassie looked across the desk at Adam Fisher, a wave of relief washed over her. She had not intended to reveal this much of herself this fast. Before meeting Adam, she would not have even thought it possible. And yet there she was, in his office, spilling her guts. It seemed almost surreal to her. She had revealed a few details to him, and then, almost without warning, the words — the *confessions* — just came pouring out of her like water through a busted dam. She had told him everything. *Everything*.

She had told him that no, she did not believe anymore. She had told him she was living a lie. She had told him she hated God for killing her son. She told him she sometimes hated Nick for still loving that God. She told him she didn't believe most of the things she said on her and Nick's TV program "Listening to God" or, for that matter, the things she said to almost anyone she knew.

And she told him about Nick, too. She told him that Nick had been exhibiting odd, compulsive behaviors. He wrote notes to remind himself of almost everything, even the most mundane details of life. Notes and lists. They were everywhere, pinned up on the walls, hung up on the fridge; everywhere she looked there were lists of five, six, seven items. It was almost as if he had lost his short-term memory — as if he barely even knew who he was anymore.

She told him all of that and more. The words flowed effortlessly because she sensed that he already knew most of these things. Almost from the instant they met, she could tell that he saw right through her. Maybe her mask only worked on people in her own narrow, religious circle. Maybe to "outsiders" she looked as phony as a three dollar bill.

And then the conversation turned to sex. She revealed how unsatisfied she was, how lonely. Desperately, painfully, hopelessly lonely. It wasn't that she did not have a physical relationship with Nick. It wasn't that Nick wasn't into her. It wasn't even that she wasn't into him. It was that she wasn't into herself. She wasn't the character she pretended to be in their relationship. And because of that, she did not enjoy sex. At all. But like with everything else in her life, she faked it. And then, when she was alone, she satisfied herself. She had an intimate relationship with her own fingers and her vibrator.

She told Adam all of this. Somehow, it was easy. He seemed to know already, to be drawing the words out of her. She had never, in all her life, spoken to someone about these things. And it felt so good. She felt more than just relieved; she felt aroused. With each intimate detail she revealed, she felt more and more excited, as if she were...*undressing* herself before him, stitch by stitch, right there in his office. She found herself becoming wet. She desperately wanted to touch herself.

She crossed her legs, knitting her hands on her knee, just below the hemline of her skirt. She could feel Adam's eyes on her calves as she spoke. He began to probe her about her sex life.

"How often do you masturbate?"
"When do you do it?"
"Where do you do it?"
"How long does it take?"
"How do you feel about it?"
"Does your husband know?"

He spoke softly, almost hypnotically. As they talked, she grew more and more excited. She crossed her legs one way, then the other, trying to put out the fire between them. But with each question—and each answer—she grew more excited. Slowly, but surely she was nearing the edge. A part of her fought it, clenching her thighs, trying to squeeze back the orgasm that was trying to break free. Another part, however, did not want to fight it. And that part was winning.

She knew if she did not leave instantly, she would embarrass herself horribly. She searched her mind for excuses, but none came. Meanwhile, Adam kept asking questions, and the sound of his voice, and the sight of his young, handsome face, kept driving her closer and closer to the edge, until finally, she could take it no more.

She had to leave. "I—I'm sorry," she stammered, looking at her watch. "I have to go." She did not even try to give a reason.

"Wait," Adam said, and got out of his chair. He put his hands on the arms of her chair and leaned forward, trapping her there. "Don't go," he whispered, his face only inches from her own. She let out a small, weak yelp, like a trapped kitten looking up at a concerned bystander.

She couldn't hold it any longer. She threw her legs open and dug her fingers into the sopping wet fabric of her panties. At the same time, she threw her other hand behind Adam's head and pulled his lips up against hers, probing intensely with her tongue. And then she came. Slowly and violently, in huge, devastating waves. When it was over, she just sat there, legs and arms akimbo, and sighed with relief.

Adam sat back in his chair. "I want to see you again," he said. "But not in my office."

She just smiled at him.

Chapter 17

Nick was dreaming. The Thing had promised to reveal to Nick where they had met before. To reveal it in his dreams. And now he was doing exactly that.

The year was 2012. The place was a church called *The Old Wooden Cross*. Nestled in the Appalachian Mountains, it was the very quintessence of the kind of snake handling, strychnine drinking, superstitious religion that people associated with poor, rural churches. Nick was there as a ploy to boost ratings. His assignment: A mass exorcism. Folks from near and far, who believed they had unclean spirits, had converged upon the small old church, hoping Nick's healing touch might be the answer to their affliction.

Nick knew all about these kinds of "possessed" people. In some churches, *everything* was blamed on Satan. It was almost a sign of piety to see Satan behind every evil in one's life. As a result, many church members came to believe they were possessed. Perhaps they even wanted to believe it, for at least it was an affliction with a cure — Exorcism.

But it made great TV. The atmosphere alone was

worth a few ratings points. Snakes, strychnine, and a small, rustic church filled with snaggle-toothed folks in raggedy clothing swept up in an orgy of sweat-soaked, ecstatic religious experience. It didn't get much better than that.

Toward the end of the service, the pastor summoned those with demons to come to the front of the church. With Willie on the sidelines, capturing it all on film, Nick approached the afflicted souls, bible in hand. One by one he dispatched the "demons" that haunted the folks arrayed before him. He did it the usual way: lying on of hands, passionate prayer, bold admonitions. They responded in the usual ways: screeching, screaming, kicking, spitting — one of them even foamed at the mouth. Nothing unusual; he'd seen it all before.

But one of them was different. He could tell immediately. He looked different. He even smelled different. He was middle-age, gaunt, with a pale, greenish complexion. He lay there, in a seated pose on the floor, staring up at him through dead, grey eyes. Eyes that seemed to be portals to another dimension. Nick approached the man. The man smiled up at him. He had a crooked smile, with several missing teeth. The man's face gleamed with sweat, as if he were in the grip of a terrible fever. His hair was a mangy, matted mess, and the sweat had soaked through his clothes. The man was Martin Monroe. Nick did not know it then, of course, and he did not know it in his dream. But he would remember when he woke up.

As Nick approached, he could swear he saw a thin mist of smoke rising off of the man's skin. He looked like a cartoon character that had swallowed a hundred hot chili peppers. Nick laid a hand on the man's head. It was like touching a light burning oven. As Nick prayed over him, the man began to change. His features seemed to melt, as if from the heat, into something else. *Someone* else. And within a few moments, Nick found himself staring, not at Martin Monroe, but at his recently deceased son, Raymond Gallo. Nick's heart leapt in his chest. His first instinct was to throw his arms around the boy, kiss him, never let him go. But he resisted. He was paralyzed. He didn't know what to do. This was the first time he had ever encountered a *real* demon.

The man with his son's face grabbed Nick and pulled him in, inches from his face, then cried, "Help me, Dad! Please help me. It's so...hot...in here." It was his son's voice, his son's face, and, worst of all, his son's eyes. It *felt* like his son.

Nick tried to break his son's grip, but he couldn't. A few moments later, Raymond let go and fell backward, onto the floor, and began writhing in pain. As he did, the smoke poured off of him, as if he were on fire. Nick fell down to his knees and cradled his son's head in his arms.

"Raymond, Raymond!" he cried, looking deep into his eyes. The smoke was thick now — thick and black, like the smoke from a rubber fire. It stung his eyes and choked him. Raymond grabbed Nick's wrists again. Nick just sat there on his knees, watching helplessly, as Raymond looked him right in the eyes and said in a weak, trembling voice: "Look at what they're doing to me."

And then suddenly Nick and his son were not in *The Old Wooden Cross* church anymore. They were someplace else entirely. A large, industrial complex of some kind. The sound of grinding metal and humming machines filled the air. The ceilings were about three stories high and the air was thick and hot and humid. Patches of smoke rose up from the ground. And milling about him, going to and fro, were large men in work clothes with tools in their hands and more in their belts. Except that they weren't men, really. They were about seven feet tall, powerfully muscled, with no necks, and faces like stone. Grim, dark faces that showed no emotion, except perhaps, a slight hint of anger.

He heard Raymond. He was crying for help. He followed the sound, strolling across the huge, smoking floor of the complex, as the sounds of the "men" working rang out all around him. He followed the sound down a narrow corridor which led to a large steel door. The door was open. He entered. There was Raymond, naked, lying down face first. Behind him stood one of the "men" — also naked. He had one massive hand on Raymond's back, pinning him to the table. In his other hand he held his huge, fully erect penis — about 12 inches in length, and as thick as baseball bat. It almost seemed to be throbbing; bulging veins stretched the skin tight as a drum. As Nick entered, the "man" looked at him and smiled. His had huge, iron teeth, spaced widely apart, and dripping with saliva.

"Help me, please!" Raymond cried out, turning his head to the side and looking at Nick. "Help me! They do this…to me…all…day…long."

The "man" let out a soft, primal grunt, then pushed his penis slowly into Raymond's rectum. Raymond shrieked with pain. The "man" gave several thrusts, then came out. His penis was dripping blood. Raymond's blood. He waited for a moment, then did it again. Again, Raymond shrieked in pain. Then another "man" entered the room from a different door. He, too, was naked. He approached Raymond from the front, prying his mouth open with his huge fingers. And then he stuck his penis in his mouth as the other man continued to penetrate him from behind. Raymond thrashed uselessly against the invasion, his screams trapped in his own throat. The other man now looked at Nick. Just like the first, he opened his mouth to reveal a set of iron teeth.

Nick watched the scene in disbelief. He put his hands to his head, closed his eyes, and screamed. And then, suddenly, he was back in *The Old Wooden Cross* church, kneeling over the trembling figure of Martin Monroe. The members of the congregation had huddled around the two men, cheering Nick on as they watched the battle. What had transpired, what they had actually seen, he had no idea.

He pulled himself together, stared into the camera, and then, without thinking, placed a hand on Martin's head, and commanded the demon to leave him. Immediately, Martin collapsed in a heap. It was over. It was over, Nick knew, because the demon was finished for now. Not because it had been cast out. But that would be their little secret. As Martin revived, seemingly in his right mind, the celebration ensued. The good guys won again; the demons were gone; everyone was happy.

Nick woke up. He was bathed in sweat. He put a hand on his forehead and sighed deeply. Now he remembered. He remembered where he had seen Martin before. And apparently, where he had seen that THING before. He recalled its words: *I have been inside of you almost as long as I've been inside of him.* Apparently, the demon had used Martin to get to him. To get inside of him. And apparently, it had been in him ever since that day. But why? What did it want with him? And what about the Blackwood house? He recalled the words of the old man just before he killed himself: *This will be great for your ratings*. Well, it was. The ratings shot up; new channels started airing his programs—both of them—*Into the Devil's Den* and *Listening to God*. Overnight, he had gone from local hit to national celebrity.

Was it the same demon? It would seem so. He was following Nick around, tracing his movements. What does he want from him? He didn't know. But he planned on finding out.

Chapter 18

Terrence looked down at the floor boards. Bathed in sweat, exhausted, and reeking, he knew he had to get out soon or he would die. Every day the temperature went up a few degrees. Every day he got closer to being roasted alive like a giant pig at a country fare. Just like all the other victims. But how to escape he hadn't a clue. The shackle on his wrist was not going to break, nor was the chain running from it to the pipe. It had to be unlocked, and only two people had the key. One of them, he knew, would never budge. Not an inch. Nor could he overpower him, especially not now in his weakened condition. The other one, however, might prove susceptible. He had seen her put the key to the shackle on the same chain as the key to the door. And she kept that key on her when she came down here to see him. So if he could grab her, he had a chance. A chance to get the key and escape.

He heard footsteps coming down the basement steps. He looked at his watch. It read 4 PM. Too early for dinner. That usually came around six. Moments later there was the sound of the key turning, and then, slowly, the door swung open. For a moment, there was no-one there — just empty space staring at him from the doorway. Then, very slowly, as if to build the anticipation, a boot came into view. A long, black boot with a stiletto heel.

What the fuck?

Next, a leg came into view. One leg. And then, slowly, in pieces, the rest of her frame appeared, until finally, it filled the doorway. There she stood, palms pressed up against the door jams on either side of the doorframe, legs stretched open in a V-stance, with a whip hanging from the belt cinched just beneath her bustier. She wore black stockings and panties and a garter belt. She had done up her face with rouge and bright red lipstick. She just stood there, filling the doorway, sliding her palms up and down against the door jams, as if messaging them. "Well," she said, as if annoyed that he had not said anything. "What do you think?"

He didn't know what to think. So, he said simply: "You look very nice."

She made a sad, pouty face, as if terribly disappointed. "Just nice?" she said. "You sure know how to flatter a girl."

She entered the room, keeping her distance as always, and took the whip out of her belt. Then she snapped it hard against the floor. "I'm going to have to teach you how to appreciate a woman," she said. "Take off your pants."

Terrence undid his belt and zipper and stripped down to his shorts. "Now the shorts," she said. He obeyed. There he stood, naked from the waist down, bathed in sweat, staring at his female captor.

She glanced down at his penis, then made a wry, disapproving look with her mouth. "Small one," she said, sounding disappointed.

Terrence said nothing. There was nothing to say. She was calling the shots, and that was it. He glanced quickly at the floor by the doorway, where she had dropped her keys. One of those keys was the key to the shackle on his wrist.

She just stood there, staring at him contemptuously, then said, "Get on your hands and knees, like a dog."

He did. And he felt like one, too. Not only because she had humiliated him, but because of why he was there in the first place. Because he had cheated on his wife — or tried to cheat — with this woman. And now, there he was, chained to a pipe, stark naked, down on all fours like a dog. Truly the prophets had spoken correctly when they said: The wages of sin is death.

"That's a good boy," she said. "Now, I want you to bark like a dog."

He obeyed.

"Again," she commanded.

Again, he obeyed.

"Louder," she shouted, cracking the whip hard against his butt.

He obeyed.

"I said *louder*," she shouted again, cracking the whip even harder. After several minutes of whipping, his butt had turned a bright red. He began to feel sick to his stomach. He stopped the barking, and curled up on the floor in a fetal position, his hands on his stomach.

"Hey, what are you doing?" Sam shouted. "I didn't say we were finished."

"I can't," he said weakly. "I'm...I'm sick."

And then he vomited. Hard. A big, ugly spray of grayish goo came pouring out of him like a geyser, spilling out all over the wooden planks. A brief respite followed, as he caught his breath, then another geyser came pouring out. Another respite followed, and then one last round. When he was done, he rolled over onto his back, gasping.

"Jesus Christ," Sam shouted. "You ruined everything, you dumb fuck!" She looked down at the mess with disgust. "Christ," she repeated, then stormed out of the room. She reappeared moments later with some dirty towels in her hand. "Clean that mess up," she growled, throwing the towels at Terrence. "And you'd better do a good job."

He struggled back to his knees and started cleaning. "You fucking prick," she snarled from the doorway. "This isn't over. We're gonna do this again, and next time you'd better not fuck it up or I won't wait for Austin to kill you; I'll do it myself!" Then she slammed the door, locked it, and went back upstairs.

Yes, thought Terrence. *We'll do it again.*

Next time, he would make his move.

Chapter 19

For the third time in three weeks, Nick Gallo sat beside Martin Monroe, prepared to match wits with that Thing that inhabited his body. This time he had come with a purpose. He wanted to find out what the hell was going on. He had some questions that needed answering, and he planned on getting them.

"The first thing I want to know," Nick said, feeling almost like he was talking to an old friend, or enemy, as the case may be, "is: What do you want with Martin Monroe?"

"Nothing," the Thing said. "I used him to get to you."

"Then why bother with him at all?"

"Do you not know my name? I am the Prince of the Power of the Air, my friend. I am in the air. Everywhere. I am a part of consciousness itself."

The Prince of the Power of the Air. Nick knew that was a name, not for a demon, but for Satan himself. "Who are you?" he asked.

"Does it matter?" the Thing replied. "Wherever my thoughts take root, there I am. Call me whatever you like."

This stunned Nick—the idea that he might be sitting across not from a demon, but from Satan himself. And yet somehow, it did not really seem to matter, at least not for his purposes. It didn't change anything.

"Okay," Nick said. "Was it you at the Blackwood house?"

The Thing was not smiling now, not being coy, or wry, or sarcastic. He was just speaking directly, as anyone else would speak. All business. No more games. Which was fine with Nick. He was tired of the games.

"Oh, yes," the Thing said. "That was me."

"What did you want?"

"I already told you; I wanted to boost your ratings."

"Why? Why do you care about my ratings?"

"Because I have big plans for your show. Big plans."

"Like what?"

"I want to use it as a stage."

"A stage for what?"

"I want you to hold a trial. A real, live trial. With attorneys and witnesses and plaintiffs and a defendant and all of that."

"And who do you want to try?"

"God, of course. I want to try God."

"Why?"

"Do you really have to ask?"

"Okay, I get it; you hate God. But do really think a trial is going to do any good?"

"I don't know, but I do think it is high time."

"High time?"

"Yes, high time. He has eluded blame long enough."

"Is that so?"

"Yes, it is. And do you know how He does it?"

"How?"

"Oh, it's the oldest trick in the book, my dear friend. Deflection. He deflects the blame."

"Onto you, I presume."

"Well, yes, that's one of His tricks. But mostly He deflects it onto *you*. Onto man."

"Is there something wrong with holding man accountable for his sins?"

"Not at all. But what about *His* sins? What I would like to know is: Why is MAN always on trial, but never God? I'll tell you why. Because He keeps man focused on individual acts, performed by individual men. And that keeps them divided. It keeps them angry at each other, blaming each other. It keeps their mind of the Big Picture, which is the fact that *He's* the one responsible for all of it. He pulls all of the strings, sets all of the circumstances, and can change things at any time, but who do men blame when things go wrong? Each other. It's disgusting!"

"I understand what you're saying," Nick said. "But putting God on trial? What good will it do? People have been blaming God for things for a thousand years. It's nothing new. What do you hope to accomplish?"

"I wish to show what a petty tyrant He is. How hateful, how implacable, how utterly, absolutely *small*. I wish to open people's eyes that they might *see* what it is they are worshipping."

Nick knew he was treading on dangerous ground. First, he could not know this Thing was really Satan. Secondly, even if he was, it did not mean he was speaking the truth, for Satan is a liar and the father of lies. He might be getting duped at this very moment. And finally, even if he was Satan, and he was telling the truth, there was still the issue of blasphemy. How could he dare to put God almighty on trial? To place man in the place of God and God in the place of man? And all at the behest of God's most solemn enemy? No, he simply could not do it.

"I cannot put God on trial," Nick said flatly.

"Your loyalty is misplaced; you do know that, don't you? Deep down?"

"I cannot put God on trial," Nick repeated.

"Yes," the Thing said, "I heard you the first time. Very well, do as you must. But know this: Until you agree to put Him on trial, I will not leave you alone. I will dog your steps and torment your soul. And Martin's, too."

"Do what you must," Nick said. With that, he stood up and left the room.

Chapter 20

Sam was in the living room watching TV when the doorbell rang. Her heart leapt at the sound. She was not expecting company and, given her situation, certainly did not want company. *Probably just a Jehovah's Witness*, she thought, getting up from the couch. *Take their pamphlet, say thank you, and send them on their way to bug somebody else.* No big deal.

She opened the door. Standing there was a short, hefty man in a gray suit. He was bald on the top of his head, with a thin layer of hair around the sides and back. He looked about 50, with a beefy face and thin, wire-rimmed glasses. "Hello, ma'am," he said. "How are you?"

"I'm fine," Sam said, wondering who this man was and what he wanted.

"Are you Samantha Gallo?" he asked.

"Yes," she said.

"Hi, I'm Sheriff Witter," he said, extending a hand. "Burt Witter."

Sam's heart skipped a beat and for a moment she actually felt dizzy. She hid it well, though—at least she hoped she did—and shook the Sheriff's hand.

151

"Hello, sheriff," she said, forcing a smile and praying he would not ask to come in. *Just how well does sound travel through those basement walls*, she wondered. *How loud do you have to scream to be heard? Why didn't Austin have that room sound proofed before he started this whole fucking thing?*

"I guess you're wondering why I'm here," the sheriff said, smiling.

"Well, yes, of course," Sam replied, feeling flush. She could already feel a thin film of sweat forming underneath her blouse as she hoped against hope that this visit was about something other than Terrence Baker and/or the recent preacher murders. Maybe some overdue traffic tickets. A driving violation. A case of mistaken identity. Maybe he was just going around warning people about an escaped con or something. Anything else would be better. Much better.

"Well," he said, making a kind of constipated face, and looking very uncomfortable. "I'm here to talk to you about something." He took a paper out of his pocket and unfolded it. "I was hoping you might be able to explain this." He showed it to her, still holding it in his own hand. It was a printout of cell phone records. "It seems like you received a call on this date..." He pointed. "...from a man named Terrence Baker." His voice had a question mark in it, as if the whole thing confused him a bit.

"I...I don't recall getting such a call," she said. She wanted to say more — *I get a lot of wrong numbers, I've never heard of the man, I don't keep track of all my calls* — but she knew the more she said, the more guilty she would look, so she resisted the urge to run off at the mouth that people get when they're nervous.

"I see," the sheriff said. During the awkward silence that ensued, her racing mind wondered if she should ask him what this was about. Would that make her sound more guilty or less guilty? What would the average person say in this circumstance? They would probably say *something*. By the time she decided to make an innocent sounding inquiry as to the nature of the question, the sheriff broke the silence. "I hope you don't mind ma'am, but would it be all right if we talked inside?"

Her heart leapt again, this time more severely than the last, and she could almost hear her entire world crumbing all around her like so many old walls in a dilapidated building. Struggling desperately to maintain her composure, she smiled and said, "Sure, come on in."

The sheriff entered the living room. Hat in hand, he strolled slowly around the room, looking all around. Sam desperately wanted to steer him away from the kitchen, where the cellar door was, but she resisted the urge. She did not want to do anything that might look suspicious. Better to let him snoop a little.

She did not hear anything coming from the basement. Maybe he hadn't heard the bell; it was a low sounding bell. Maybe he was even asleep when it rang. Or too sick to hear it. Or too sick to scream. Or maybe he was even dead. Whatever the case, if he had heard it, he would be screaming by now, and he wasn't, so everything was cool. All she had to do was keep the conversation as low as possible so he wouldn't hear them talking.

She stood in the living room, by the couch, as the sheriff moved about the room. She hoped that by not following him she would encourage him to stay in that vicinity of the room, away from the kitchen. He walked back over toward her. She did not ask if he would like to sit down. She didn't want him to get comfortable.

"The reason I asked you about the phone call," he

said, "is that I'm investigating a disappearance." He paused, as if waiting for her reaction.

"Okay," she said simply.

The sheriff continued, "The man who disappeared is.... Well the same person who called you on the day he went missing."

The sheriff seemed genuinely uncomfortable, as if he regretted having to bother her about this. It seemed to her that he did not believe she had committed this crime. Probably because she was a woman. Women didn't commit those kinds of crimes. They just didn't, and the sheriff knew it.

"Anyhow," the sheriff said, "it's probably nothing, probably just a wrong number, but...I gotta check out every lead, you know?"

"Of course," she agreed, firmly deciding to say as little as possible. That was her strategy; it seemed to be working, so she should probably stick with it.

"Anyway," the sheriff continued, "do you know anything about that call?"

"I don't," Sam said, shrugging. "I'm sorry; I wish I could be of more help."

"Well, that's okay," the sheriff smiled. "No harm done. Like I said, I just have to check every lead, that's all."

"I understand," she said. To her relief, the sheriff headed for the door. She opened it for him.

"Thank you for your time, ma'am," he said as he left.

"You're welcome," she replied. Then she closed the door, pressed up against it with her back, looked up at the ceiling, and breathed a huge sigh of relief. That was a close one. Too close.

She headed for the phone and called Austin.

Chapter 21

Nick woke up at 6:00 A.M. and looked at the list on his dresser. It read:

1. Get up
2. Brush teeth

That was all he needed for now. The next twenty-five items on the list could wait; first he had to brush his teeth. First things first. He slid quietly out of bed, so as to not wake up Cassie, put on his bathrobe and slippers, and strolled down the hallway to the bathroom.

He had a busy day ahead. He had to meet with his producer to discuss plans for upcoming broadcasts of his two shows, both of which were now bona-fide hits. Then he had to work on a sermon for Sunday. Then he had to call Adam to discuss Martin's condition, and plan his next move. Then he had to do an interview with a local news reporter. Then he had to answer about a zillion emails. Then he had another interview. Then he had to meet with a parishioner about an important personal matter. And that was just some of what he had on his plate that day.

He looked in the mirror. He had bags under both eyes. That did not surprise him. Sleep had become a rare commodity lately. He picked up the toothpaste and squeezed a big glob onto his toothbrush and started brushing. He spit into the sink and noticed some red mixed in with the water and toothpaste. Not a good sign.

He bared his teeth in the mirror and leaned in for a closer look. Staring back at him from the mirror were two rows of big iron teeth, like the ones the men in the work-suits had. He leapt back from the mirror, a hand covering his mouth.

What the fuck?

No, it couldn't be. He was seeing things. The vision had stayed with him; the images were seared in his brain and were causing him to see things. It wasn't real. His teeth were not iron. They were regular, white, human teeth. When he took his hand off his mouth, he would see that.

He stepped up to the mirror again, placing his face about a foot in front of the glass. His hand was still on his mouth. He was afraid to take it off. What if it wasn't in his mind? Or what if it was in his mind, but he couldn't get it out? Maybe he was just going crazy.

Stop it! Stop it! he told himself, shaking his head, like a boxer trying to shake the cobwebs after taking a solid blow. It *is* your imagination, he told himself. And then, slowly, he removed his hand and bared his teeth. They were white. White as the snow. Well, not *that* white, but they were pretty white. Definitely human teeth. And yet…something was off. He dipped his head to one side to get a better angle, and touched his front teeth with his forefinger. They felt strange. He moved the finger around, as if messaging his teeth. It felt almost as if they were…moving. But that was impossible, of course. He felt again, this time with his thumb and forefinger, pressing them against his teeth, feeling for movement. He felt it again. The movement. His teeth were...vibrating.

He stood back from the mirror and shook his head again. *This couldn't be. Teeth weren't made of iron and they didn't vibrate. This was all imagination.* He took a deep breath and approached the mirror again. Again, he leaned in and put his fingers on his teeth. And once again he could feel his fingers moving against the vibration. Quite definitely. No imagination. His teeth were vibrating.

He bared his teeth more fully, like a wolf preparing to attack its prey, and ran his fingers along his them, pressing against them, trying to stop them from moving. But it only grew stronger. In fact, now he could actually *see* his teeth vibrating, as if they were all connected by some kind of invisible energy charge that was making them jump around in his mouth. He pressed at them with his hands, hoping that somehow that would help. It didn't, of course. In fact, they were vibrating even faster now. He watched helplessly as his teeth took on a life of their own. With each second now, they picked up some force, as if powered by a circuit that was growing in wattage.

Nick could not believe his eyes. This couldn't be happening. His teeth were almost spinning in his gums now; he grabbed the sides of his mouth with his hands. Blood began to drip from his mouth. Specks of red dripped down into the white porcelain sink. He put his fingers on either side of his lips and stretched them back and up, fully exposing his entire mouth. He watched, transfixed with horror, as his two rows of teeth trembled like tree leaves caught in a hurricane cross wind. And then, one by one, in rapid succession, they fell out, each one clacking into the sink in its own little pool of blood, until, after a few short moments, the sink was full of teeth. Nick just stood there, disbelieving, staring at his bloody toothless face in the mirror. Then he screamed.

"Nick?" Cassie said. "Are you okay?"

Nick shot up in bed, his T-shirt soaked with sweat. He grabbed at his mouth, probing inside. He felt them. He felt his teeth—all thirty-two of them, including four molars. They were still there, still intact, in his mouth, where they belonged. He breathed a sigh of relief and fell back into the pillow. "Oh, God," he said, "I had the worst dream."

"It must have been," Cassie said. "You're soaked with sweat."

As she tried to comfort him, he recalled the words of the Thing: *Very well, do as you must. But know this: Until you agree to put Him on trial, I will not leave you alone. I will dog your steps and torment your soul. And Martin's, too.*

On that he was proving to be a man of his word.

Chapter 22

Sam walked down the basement steps, a roll of rope and the whip in her hands. That prick had ruined something she had been looking forward to for days. A few slaps on the ass and the little wimp pukes his guts out. No fun at all. He would have to pay for that. Dearly. And that visit from the cops did not help. That *really* pissed her off. She was angry and someone had to pay. It might as well be him.

She opened the large wooden door, put the key in her pocket, and stood there in the doorway, hands on her hips, looking at her captive, as he sat there, helpless, on the bench. She almost felt sorry for him, the poor bastard. Almost. Except for one thing. He was a preacher. And he deserved to be punished.

"Well," she sighed, "here we are again." He just stared at her blankly. He looked a little green around the gills, but otherwise he seemed to be holding up okay. That was something she would have to change. She would change it, but not too fast. First, she wanted to have some fun.

"Lay down," she ordered him. "Face down."

He obeyed.

"Now put your hands behind you."

He obeyed.

She knelt down and tied his wrists together, working around and over the shackle. As she tied him up, she said: "This time I plan on getting up close and personal with you, and I can't have you trying anything naughty."

She liked the whip, but it was so...impersonal. She wanted to feel him with her own hand this time. In his weakened condition, with his hands bound, he did not pose a serious threat. He could not overpower her in that state. If he tried, she would make him sorry he did. Of course, if Austin knew the risk she was taking, he would flip. But that was okay; he didn't have to know. She wanted to have her fun, and that was it.

"Okay, up," she ordered.

He got up.

"Now, come here," she said, guiding him toward the bench. She sat down; he stood right in front of her, his waist even with her face. She unbuttoned his pants and pulled them down. She put a hand on his crotch, feeling it through the underwear. Then she pulled the underwear down. "Okay," she said, "let's see what we've got here." She cupped her hand around his ball sack and gave it a little squeeze. Then she stroked his shaft with her thumb. "Hmmm...." she said, quizzically, like a doctor intrigued by her subject. "I think we can work with this." She leaned forward and licked his penis. Just one quick, soft lick, like you would lick an ice cream cone.

"God, it's hot in here," she said, standing up. She took her shirt off and tossed it on the floor. Then the pants. Underneath she wore a black, push-up bra and black, thong panties.

"Like whatchya see?" she asked him, tickling his chin

with her fingers. She turned around in a circle, giving him a nice view of her butt cheeks. He just stood there, frozen, saying nothing.

"It's okay," she said, tickling his chin again. "You'll loosen up."

She sat back down on the bench. "Okay, come on," she said, slapping her lap, as if calling a dog. "I'm gonna give you a spanking."

He knelt over her lap. She put a hand on his butt and caressed it. He had a nice, firm ass. Small dick, but a great ass. And a pretty good body, too. She was going to enjoy this. Already she could feel herself getting wet between her legs. Yes, this was going to be fun.

She gave him a slap. Just one, tiny little slap. "Tell, me, preacher man," she said, "have you ever been spanked before? Do you enjoy it? Hmmm...? Not talking? Okay, suit yourself, but you're being a *bad* boy."

She slapped him again, this time a little bit harder. She pressed down on his rump, enjoying the way his dick felt on her lap. And if she was not mistaken, she did detect some movement down there. Barely perceptible, but something. That was good. She wanted an active — or a passive — participant. But either way, she wanted a rise out of him.

She slapped him again, this time a little harder. "How's that feel? Do you like that?" she asked.

He didn't answer.

"I'll tell you what," she said. "You be a good boy and give me what I want, and I'll turn the heat off tonight and give you a big dinner. How's that sound?"

"That sounds good," he answered weakly.

"Good!" she said. "Then we have an agreement. So, here's what I want. I want you to keep asking me to spank you harder. Beg me. No matter how hard I spank, keep pleading with me to do it harder. Can you do that?"

"Yes," he answered.

"Are you sure?" she asked, messaging his butt. "I'm really gonna slap you hard."

"I'm sure," he said.

"Okay, then, here goes!"

She started spanking him softly and slowly. "How's that? Is that good?" she asked.

"Harder," he said.

"Harder? Yeah…. You sure?"

"Uh huh. Harder."

"Okay." She slowly increased the force of the slaps. "There ya go. Is that better?"

"Harder," he said.

"Harder?" she repeated. "Oh, my, you must have really been a bad boy! Have you?"

"Yes," he said.

"Yes, what?" she asked, increasing the force some more.

"Yes, I've been a bad boy." She smacked him hard now. Real hard.

"What have you done?" she asked.

"I did a lot of things," he answered. He sounded weak and broken. That really turned her on. She was getting some serious tingling sensations now.

"Like what?" she asked, continuing to spank away.

"I cheated on my wife," he answered.

"Okay," she said. "Keep saying *harder*, remember?"

"Harder!" he said. She complied. She was spanking him *real* hard now.

"What else did you do?" she asked.

"I…I was a hypocrite. Harder!"

"How so?"

"I told people to do things that I didn't do!" he cried. "Harder!"

"Like what?" she asked, slapping his ass as hard as she could. His butt was getting very red now.

"Like...like...." He was fighting back tears. "I told people to be faithful. To love their wives. To be loyal. And I wasn't. I was...I was a hypocritical, lying, sanctimonious bag of shit! Harder! Harder!"

He seemed genuinely angry at himself. And it did not seem like an act. Sam was a great actress; she knew acting when she saw it. This was not acting. It was genuine sorrow.

For the first time, Sam saw him as a human being. A prick, maybe, but a prick who had come to realize he was a prick. "That's good!" she said, smacking him with all her might. "Confession is good for the soul." She closed her eyes and took a deep breath. She was so excited right now. So very excited.

"Harder!" he shouted.

She was swinging her hand in a sweeping arcs now, pounding him with all her might. Each smack produced a cry of pain. And each cry made her more and more excited. All the while he just kept pleading: "Harder! Harder! Harder!" He wanted to be punished. He hated himself. In fact, she realized he hated himself as much as she had hated him. And everything she had hated *about* him, he now hated *about* himself. He had come to see himself as *she* saw him. And he hated what he saw. Hated it. And she found it almost unbearably arousing.

She continued the beating, smacking him hard and fast now, grunting with each slap, the way some tennis players grunted each time they hit the ball. And with each slap, he shouted "Harder! Harder!" They were in rhythm now, the punisher and the criminal, each fully engaged in their own roles, each playing their part perfectly.

She had broken him. Mentally, emotionally, and physically. Slowly, but surely his voice began to crack.

She decided to go for the kill, raking his ravaged buttocks with a furious barrage of thudding, angry blows. Each blow sent a shock wave through her hand and arm, causing her to wince as she unleashed her full fury on her victim's battered buttocks. But she kept it up, grunting and pounding and wincing as she kicked her assault into double overdrive. *Vomp! Vomp! Vomp! Vomp!* Each blow produced a cry of pain; each cry was weaker, more anguished than the last. He was breaking. *Vomp! Vomp! Vomp! Vomp! Vomp! Vomp! Vomp!*

And then he broke down, sobbing uncontrollably, like a chastised child on his mommy's lap. She took a deep breath, relieved that it was finally over. Her arm hurt like heck. She gently eased him to the floor, propping his back up against the bench, and cradling him in her arms. "There, there," she said. "It's okay." He buried his face in her breasts, sobbing.

"I was so bad!" he cried. "I was so bad!"

She held his head against her breast. "It's okay," she whispered. "It's okay. You know now. You understand now."

He looked her deep in the eyes. "Yes," he said, his face wet with tears. "I understand now." She took his face in her hands, sliding her fingers up and down his cheeks, and drew his lips toward her own.

"Yes," she whispered. "You understand now."

She kissed him. Her whole body tingled, from her head down to her toes. She had to fight to keep from coming right then and there. She slid her hand between his legs and started rubbing. Instantly, he became hard. He was into it now; this made her even more excited. She felt like she was about to explode. And from the looks of things, so was he. She messaged him low on the shaft, to make sure he didn't come yet. He groaned with pleasure. She kissed him again, probing his mouth with her tongue. They groaned in unison, building toward a climax. The smell of her sex and their sweat filled the air. "Oh, God!" he cried as she stroked his shaft. Slowly, she moved her hand closer and closer to the head. His whole body shivered and convulsed; his penis was as hard as steel. He was right on the edge, just about to explode. And so was she.

Then, suddenly, she recoiled, and a wry, sad look crept into her face. "Uh uh," she said. "Ladies first." She stood up and pushed his head back. "Open your mouth!" she commanded, standing over him with her legs spread apart and her pussy positioned just over his mouth. Then she stuck her fingers inside and began masturbating herself. "*Unnnnhhhh!*" she cried, dipping her hips, making sure her pussy was just an inch or so from his mouth. "Oh.... Yeah.... Yeah.... *Unnnnnnnnhhhhhhhh!*" she cried out, her face contorted with agonized pleasure, as she came, squirting into his mouth. Within a few moments, it was over.

She took several deep breaths, then stepped back and slumped to the floor, a few feet from Terrence, and folded her legs, Indian style. "Oh, God, that felt good," she sighed, running a hand down her neck. She was soaked. Terrence spit the cum out of his mouth and just stared at her, looking confused. "What?" she said, smiling. "Did you really think I was going to let you come?"

She did not know that he had slipped out of the poorly-tied knot of the rope around his wrists. "What's the matter?" she asked, sticking her lower lip out in a child-like pout. "Are you mad at me? Hmmm?" She looked at him with mock sympathy. "Did you think I was gonna let you go? Huh? Is that what you thought?" She crawled over to him, putting her face in his, and spoke in a soft, gentle whisper. "Don't you know you've been a bad boy? Hmmm...." She tickled his chin with her fingers, then put her lips close to his ear, and whispered, "You have to be punished. I...hope...you...understand." Then she licked his ear, drew her head back, and smiled.

The next thing she knew, he was on her. She screamed with surprise and scrambled to her feet, trying to get to the door. He grabbed her by the waist and flung her down. She crashed against the wooden floor and screamed again, as much from fear as from pain. Again, she tried to scramble to her feet, but he cut her arms out from under her, sending her face crashing into the wooden planks. For the third time she screamed, this time from pain. As he tried to pin her down, she flailed furiously with her arms, scratching his eyes. That gave her just enough time to scramble to her feet again. But just as she started to regain her footing, Terrence slammed into her with all his might, sending her head crashing into the steel pipe. It made a sickening thudding sound. Her eyes rolled back in her head. Then she slumped slowly to the floor, like a boxer slumping down on the ropes. Terrence stood over her, gasping. She was out like a light. He looked around, pondering his next move. He grabbed her clothes off the floor, fished the keys out her pocket, and unlocked the shackle. Then he put in on her wrist. "Looks like the tables have turned," he said. "Now I'm going to have some fun with you."

Stephen Campana

Chapter 23

Nick and Cassie sat across from each other in a booth at the Bear's Claw restaurant. Nick looked admiringly at her. She looked beautiful. This was their first night out in months. Actually, it was really more of a business meeting. They were to be joined by Todd Miller, the producer of his TV show *Listening to God*, in order to discuss the possibility of staging a Trial on their show. Nick still did not like the idea, but, at Cassie's prompting, he had begun to at least entertain the possibility.

She knew what he was going through—with Martin, the Thing, the nightmares—and she wanted it to end. If that meant putting God on trial, then so be it. After all, weren't people always putting God on trial, in a sense? Isn't that what they did every time they discussed why He allows so much evil in the world? Wouldn't a trial just be an extension of a dialogue that has persisted for thousands of years?

The waitress came over to take their order. "Nothing yet," Cassie said with a smile. "We're waiting for someone."

"Sure," the waitress said. She was a thin young girl,

about 20 or so, with a pleasant smile and her hair tied up in a big, tight bun. "Hey, are you Nick Gallo?"

"Yes, ma'am," Nick smiled and said. She turned to Cassie and said, "And you must be Cassie Gallo."

"That's me."

"I watch your shows. Big fan."

They thanked her. She scampered off to the next table.

"We're big celebrities, now," Cassie said.

"Yeah," Nick replied, none too happily. What he felt like saying was: "Yeah, that Thing saw to that," but he held his tongue. He had told Cassie all about the Thing, but she did not seem entirely convinced, so he thought it best not to bring it up.

A few moments later, Todd arrived. "Hey, guys," he said, sliding in the booth next to Cassie. "Sorry I'm late."

Nick looked at his watch. "You're not late," he said. "We're early."

"Oh," Todd said. "Then I feel better." The three of them shared a laugh. Nick felt good laughing. Laughter had been in short supply lately. After some small talk, Nick decided to launch into the reason for the meeting. He had mentioned it to Todd over the phone, but Todd wanted to discuss it in person.

"So, Todd," Nick said, "what do you think of my idea?"

"Well," Todd said, "it is interesting. But it's also a very...broad idea."

"Broad?" Nick said.

"Well, what I mean is that it covers an awful lot of ground."

The waitress came over again, notepad in hand. "Can I get you guys some drinks now?" Cassie and Nick ordered Sprites; Todd ordered a club soda. When the waitress left, Todd picked up where he had left off. "What I mean is: It's not like putting a man on trial. For instance, let's say John Q. is on trial for killing his mother-in-law."

"You mean that's illegal?" Nick joked.

His response prompted a swift kick in the shins from Cassie under the table. Todd laughed. "Anyhow," he continued, "to establish John Q's guilt is a simple proposition. You must establish one thing: Did he do it?"

"Right," Nick said. He suspected he knew where Todd was going with this.

"There are not a lot of variables involved," Todd continued. "Not in answering the question: Did he do it? Either he did or he didn't. If he did, he's guilty; if he didn't, he's not. End of story."

"But with God it's not so simple," Nick said.

"Exactly," Todd replied. "Think about it. Not even theologians agree on how much autonomy God exercises over human affairs. Some would say *everything* happens according to His will; others would say only some things. There's no consensus. I'm not even sure what it *means* to find God guilty. Does it mean that He *caused* something bad, or that He *is* bad? Can He *cause* something bad *without* being bad, as many theologians believe?"

"I see what you mean?" Nick said. "How do you try God without engaging in a long, complicated theological discussion?"

"Exactly," Todd answered.

"I don't know," Nick agreed.

"And that's not all," Todd said. "What will the charge be? One who believes God has mishandled His world might charge Him with any number of counts ranging from negligence to murder to genocide. And what about witnesses? What about rules of evidence? Is hearsay permitted? And what qualifies as hearsay with regard to God? Is the bible hearsay? These are just a few of the things we will have to iron out before proceeding."

"Perhaps we will have to assemble a team of legal experts to consult with," Nick suggested.

"Most definitely," Todd agreed. "And what about a judge and jury? And how do we decide on a jury? A jury is supposed to consist of one's peers. As far as I know, God doesn't have any."

Nick waved up a hand of surrender. "I get it. I get it. This is going to take some doing." But what he was really thinking was: I have to find out what the hell the Thing wants, and try to work it out with it. That's the only reason it was even considering this in the first place.

Chapter 24

Terrence sat there on the bench waiting for Sam, now sprawled out on the floor and chained to the pipe, to come to. He couldn't wait to see her face. He couldn't wait to see her reaction when she suddenly realized the tables had been completely turned. That now she was *his* prisoner. This was the kind of moment people dreamed about their whole lives. What would she say? Would she beg? Cry? Try to make a deal? What would she do now that he held all the cards? Oh, it was almost too good to be true. And that first instant—that would be the best. He wished he could capture it on film and replay it every day for the rest of his life.

She began to stir. Here it was—his moment. He sat there, leaning forward, looking right at her. He wanted his face to be the first thing she saw. She woke up and looked around, looked at herself, naked, and then, with horror, she looked at him. He said nothing. He wanted her to speak first. To his delight, she did. "I guess you're going to kill me, huh?" she said.

"Kill you?" Terrence repeated. "Why, I hadn't thought of that. What would you do with you if you were me?"

"Look," she snarled, "I'm not going to play your game. You win; I lose. I get it. But I'm not going to beg you. Do whatever the fuck you want."

"Oh, I intend to, my dear," Terrence smiled. He just stared at her for a bit, savoring the moment, before continuing. When he spoke again, it was in a calm, conversational tone, as if chatting with an old friend. "You know my first job was in a clothing store. And in this upper room they kept a bunch of mannequins, some male, some female. Well, I always used to look at those female mannequins and think: Wouldn't it be great if I could just bring one to life. My own living mannequin to do *anything* I wanted with. *Anything.*"

His lips curled into a wolfish grin. "Well, now, I've got one. My own living, breathing mannequin to do anything I want with."

He chuckled malevolently. "It's almost too good to be true. Truth is: I don't know *what* to do with you. I mean: What to do first, that is. I'm going to fuck you; that goes without saying. And I'm going to lay some really intense pain on you, you know, really make you scream; I think that also goes without saying. But what to do *first*...." He shrugged his shoulders and shook his head. "I haven't got a clue."

She said nothing. Her face was a mask of defeat and resignation.

"Not that it really matters what I do," Terrence continued. "It can only end one of two ways for you now. Death or life in prison. Which one would you prefer, if you don't mind my asking?"

She did not answer. "Suit yourself," he shrugged. He paused for a few moments, then said: "You know what really pissed me off the most. When you pretended to care. That was really low. If it hadn't been for that, I would just call the cops right now and not lay a finger on you. But playing me that way, that was just fucking nasty. I want you to pay for that."

He stood up and left the room. After rummaging around the basement for a few minutes, he returned with a steel pipe, about eighteen inches in length, in his hand. He sat back down on the bench. "I think this will do just fine," he said, closing his hands around the center of the pipe, and sliding them back and forth.

"What do you think?" he asked Sam. "Are you up for some more spanking?"

She said nothing.

"Okay," he said, leaning forward, elbows on his knees. "Here are the rules. I want you to be an active participant in this. Otherwise, I'm just spanking a corpse, and that does nothing for me, understand?"

No response.

"So, here's the deal. You're going to have to react. When I spank you, I want you to yell 'Harder.' But not just that: I want you to pretend it's getting you off. Hurting you and getting you off at the same time. Do you understand? And groan a lot. Sexual sounding groans. You know: *Unnnnnnhhhhh* and *Ahhhh* and that sort of thing. Okay?"

Silence.

He was getting impatient. "Now, look, we can do this one of two ways. I can take this pipe and ram it up your ass, tearing your internal organs apart, and leaving you an invalid for the rest of your life. Or, you can get on my lap. So, which one is it gonna be?"

He slapped his naked thigh. "Come on, now. Up! Up!"

She climbed to her feet and slumped over his lap. Her body seemed limp, lifeless, defeated. He liked that. It made him hard almost instantly. He put a hand on her firm, round buttocks, and moved it in slow, gentle circles. She was really quite a specimen. He could almost forgive himself for falling for her in the first place.

"Good girl," he said. "Now, I have to warn you; this isn't going to be the kind of patty cake so-called spanking that you gave me. No, ma'am. This is going to be the real deal."

He smacked her butt softly with the steel pipe to drive home the point.

"You get what I'm saying?" He put the pipe beside him on the bench as he spoke. He wanted to start with his hand. He wanted to feel his hand on her flesh. He wanted to feel what it was like to smack her as hard as he could. "You're too quiet," he said, smacking her rump. "Remember what I said about participation."

"Harder," she said weakly.

"Come on!" He slapped her ass. "Say it like you mean it. And pretend to be getting off on it."

When she didn't respond, he decided that she needed some prodding. Literally. He held the pipe up against her rectal cavity, held it for a moment, then began pushing it in.

"Okay, okay!" she yelled immediately. "I'll do it!"

"Good girl," Terrence said. "I'm glad we understand each other."

He put the pipe down and smacked her again. Hard.

"Harder!" she said.

Terrence grinned with satisfaction. She was coming around. He hit her again. And again. And again. *Vomp. Vomp. Vomp.* Each one a little harder than the last. The loud, clapping sound his hand made against her soft, round buttocks was like music to his ears.

"You're doing very well, now," he said. "Keep it up. And don't forget: This is turning you on. Come on; sell it to me."

His words put him in mind of something he heard said once: Sincerity is everything; if you can fake that, you've got it made. He laughed at the thought, then continued the beating.

"Harder," Sam groaned, her voice brimming with feigned arousal. Except that it didn't sound feigned. Terrence was impressed. He was smacking her hard now. Very hard. Her butt was bright red, and he knew she had to be hurting. He cranked it up even more, throwing everything behind each shot.

Vomp! Vomp! Vomp! Vomp!

With each shot, she squealed with pain, then shouted, "Harder! Harder!"

Vomp! Vomp! Vomp!

"Ouuuuchhhh! Harder! Harder! Unnnnhhhh! Harder!"

"I can't do it any harder!"

"Oh, please," she begged. "Harder!"

He took the pipe in his hand. "Okay, you asked for it." He brought the pipe down hard against her already red and raw buttocks.

"Ouucchhh!" she squealed. "Unnnhhhh! Harder!"

"Are you sure?" he asked, smacking her hard with the pipe. "I mean: Are you really enjoying this, or just pretending?"

"No," she moaned, "I really am."

"You want me to keep it up?"

"Yes. Yes, please!"

Vomp! "Like that?"

"Yeah, oh yeah. More. More! Unnnnhhhhhh!"

Her voice was getting weaker and weaker. She was in agony. His dick was harder than the pipe he was using to pulverize her buttocks.

Vomp! Vomp! Vomp! Vomp!

"Ouuuucchhhhh! Oh, don't stop. Don't stop!"

"I think you've had enough,"

"No. No, please! Don't stop. Unnnnnhhhhhhh! Please! Unnnnnhhhhhh!"

"Are you sure?"

"Yes!"

She was forcing the words out now, barely able to speak. Her butt was a mangled mess of welts and bruises, some of which were bleeding. Terrence could only imagine how badly she wanted to stop begging him to hurt her, and start begging him to stop instead. A small, dark smile crept into his face at the thought.

Vomp! Vomp! Vomp! Vomp!

Her screams of agony were really turning him on.

"Harder!" she forced herself to say, gasping.

"Why do you want me to do it harder?"

Vomp!

"Ouuuuchhhhh! Because I like it!"

"Why do you like it?"

Vomp!

"It...." Her voice was fading now. She could barely speak.

"I can't hear you! Why do you like it?"

"Because...It feels so...good. It makes me so...excited."

"How excited?"

"Real, real excited. Like I'm...going...to...come.

Unnnnnhhhhh!"

"But you can't come if I don't keep spanking you, right?"

"Right!"

"But I really do think you've had enough."

"No, keep spanking me! Please! Just…until…I…come. Please. Unnnnhhhh!"

"Well, okay. How many more do you need?"

"Just…three or four."

"All right, here goes." *Vomp!*

"Ohhhhh! Yeah. Harder!" *Vomp!*

"Ohhhhh! Oh, yeah. I'm…almost…there! One more!"

"I think I'd better stop now."

"No, please! One more. Please, just…let…me…come!"

"Sure, you can come. But me first."

He tossed her off his lap, and onto the hard floor. "Get on your back."

She obeyed, grimacing as the raw flesh of her flayed buttocks pressed against the hardwood of the floor planks.

"Good girl," Terrence said. "Now, open your mouth."

As she opened her mouth, he squatted over her, stroking his throbbing penis. Just as he was about to come Sam said, "Wait." Then she reached out with one hand, and gently guided his penis into her mouth.

"Oh, yeah," Terrence said, as her lips closed around him and her tongue messaged his shaft. "Oh, that feels good," he moaned. "Oh, God… Unnnnnhhhhhh!"

He was coming. Unfortunately, his orgasm was cut short by an incredible stab of pain. He screamed with agony as Sam's teeth clamped down on his dick like a Pit Bull's jaws on a child's arm. He thrashed wildly, trying to break free, but she would not let go. Blood shot out everywhere, spraying the floor planks, as his screams reverberated through the tiny room.

Finally, after what seemed like forever, she let go. He went flying backward, arms flailing wildly, into the opposite wall. Standing there, he stared in horror at Sam, who had the lower half of his penis in between her teeth. She spit it out like a peach pit. There it sat, in a puddle of blood, on the wood floor, halfway between the two of them. He stared at it disbelievingly, then at his own mangled dick, truncated like a tree stump, the vessels and veins hanging out like roots. It dripped blood like a leaky faucet.

The two said nothing for a moment, as he leaned against the wall, gasping with pain and terror.

Sam spoke first. "Listen to me," she said firmly. "Are you listening?"

He looked at her, his face a mask of horror.

"Are you listening?" she repeated.

"Yes," he said.

"We can fix this," she said. "We can fix this so that no-one dies and no-one goes to prison. And you can even get your dick sowed back on."

He was listening. "Here's what we're going to do," she said. "You're going to take the key and get me out of this shackle. Then we're both going to get dressed. Then I'm going to pack your dick up in ice and put it in a container. And then I'm going to drive you to the hospital. Is that okay with you?"

He nodded affirmatively.

"Then, let's go," she said.

He dragged himself to his feet, his hand clutching his mangled stump of a dick, and then, groaning with pain, he fetched the key and unshackled her. They got dressed in a hurry, each keeping an eye on the other as they slid into their clothes. Then they hurried upstairs, packed his penis in ice, then ran out to the car. She started it up, pulled out, and took off for the nearest hospital.

Neither spoke on the ride there, although Terrence's cries of pain were a constant reminder of the hideous ordeal they had just put each other through. She pulled into the emergency entrance, stopped, and said, "This is where it ends for us. You get patched up and go home. End of story. Tell anyone about me and you're ruined. You will have to explain to the cops why you had your dick in my mouth, how you got lured there in the first place, and you will be found out. Found out and ruined. The best thing for you to do is get patched up, and go on with your life."

He nodded. "Go," she said, turning her eyes away from him. He opened the door and stumbled off toward the emergency entrance doors, clutching the container in his hands.

She drove off, her heart still pounding. But she didn't have to worry about him. He wouldn't talk. She knew people well enough to know that.

Nothing buys silence like shame.

Stephen Campana

Chapter 25

"This is so wrong," Cassie said, nestled in Adam's arms on his sofa.

"You're right," he said. "It is."

"Am I terrible person for doing this?" she asked.

"Probably," Adam said.

She playfully elbowed him in the ribs. "Thanks a lot," she said.

But that's what she liked about him. He was honest. He called it like he saw it, be it good, bad, or ugly. And that was something she had not experienced in decades. In fact, she had not experienced real honesty since before she became a "born again" Christian. Not with others and not with herself. Around Adam she could just be herself. Around him she felt about a thousand pounds lighter. And she needed that—at least for a while. Needed to relax. Needed to face who she was. Otherwise, she would go mad. Especially now with all that was going on: her and Nick's newfound celebrity status, Nick's increasingly odd behavior, and of course, his insistence that Satan had now taken a personal interest in him. It had all become rather overwhelming. She needed somewhere to escape.

And for now, that somewhere was in Adam's arms.

"So, tell me about Martin Monroe," she said.

Adam sighed. "Martin's like a lot of people I come across. He has problems, and Satan is a convenient foil."

"Do you think there really could be a Satan? A God? A spiritual dimension to our lives?"

"I don't know what that means — Spirit. I think it's just a word we give to the unknown. As soon as something is known, it's not spirit anymore; it's science."

"But we can never know everything."

"Of course not, but that doesn't mean it's spirit. It just means we haven't identified everything yet."

"Have you identified what is wrong with Martin?"

"I think so. I think there are a few things wrong with him."

"Such as?"

"Guilt, for one. I think he carries a load of guilt around with him. Fear also. I think he's a very frightened person. So, he has convinced himself that he's possessed by demons. This accomplishes two things. First, it helps him make sense of what's going on in his mind. It gives it an explanation. And second, it gives him the hope of a simple cure. Exorcize the demon and everything will be okay."

"But life's not always so simple, right?"

"Right. The mind is very complex. One human brain — one grey bundle of nerve cells sitting in your skull — is more complex than the entire universe. People don't like that. That would prefer simple answers. They would like to believe things are black and white. Good people do good things. Bad people do bad things. God is good; Satan is bad. The good go to heaven; the wicked go to hell. God made the world in six days. Children die because God needs more angels. There's a reason for everything. What doesn't kill us makes us stronger. All dogs go to heaven. Blah, blah, blah, blah...."

"So, what does it all come down to in the end?"

"We live; we die, and everything in between is pot luck."

"That's an incredibly depressing world view."

"Yes, it is. I sometimes wish I didn't believe it."

Cassie sighed. "At least you *know* what you believe. I don't. I envy you. Hell, I envy Nick, too. He knows what he believes."

"Does he?"

Cassie thought about it for a moment, then said, "Yeah, I think he does. He has his doubts like all of us, but for the most part, yeah, I think he does."

"Then good for him," Adam said. He said it without sarcasm.

"Yeah, good for him," Cassie said.

She closed her eyes as Adam ran his fingers up and down her arms. "Ummm, that feels nice," she sighed.

She wondered if she would ever again know what she believed.

Chapter 26

Sam and Austin sat across from each other in the living room of Sam's home. She had just finished telling him everything. She had told him about her foray into S & M. Her dreams. Her experiment with being a mistress. She told him about how Terrence had turned the tables on her. How she bit his dick off. And finally, about how it all ended up: with the two of them, wounded and bleeding, parting ways in a hospital parking lot, with an agreement to leave it all behind them forever. That's what she told him, and now, she sat there, awaiting his reaction, and praying he would not be too upset. To her amazement, he seemed rather placid about the whole thing. He just shrugged his shoulders and said: "These things happen. Live and learn, right?"

"Right," she said.

Then he said: "I want to show you something," and took a newspaper clipping out of his pocket and handed it to her. It was titled: *Is The War on Religion Succeeding?*

It read:

While most people have nothing but contempt for the War on Religion killer and his sick vendetta, it seems that his message is resonating with some people. Some have gone so far as to brand him a "prophet" and to openly support his cause, heeding his words to use violence against clergy people. That's right; people are actually wounding, maiming, and killing in the name of this twisted cause — the cause of destroying Religion. A few examples:

5/11/2015 North Carolina A man and his girlfriend, high on cocaine, kidnap a Baptist preacher. They drive him to a remote wooded area, about a mile from where they live, strip him, and tie him to a stake. Then they pour honey on him and open a bee hive on the ground in front of him. They watch as he is devoured by the hungry bees.

6/15/2015 New York City A gang of youths — two of them gay, one transsexual — murder a priest in Central Park, pounding him with sticks and rocks, and caving in his skull, before fleeing the area.

7/20/2015 Los Angeles A man crouches near the window of an abandoned home, situated across the street from a Baptist church. When the church lets out, he opens fire on the people, spraying them with bullets from his AK-47. Two are killed and twelve wounded.

Those are just a few examples. There are more. It is sad, but the simple fact is that this madman's message has found more than a few sympathetic ears.

Sam handed Austin the clipping back, smiling weakly. "That's great," she said.

"Great?" Austin said. "It's fantastic! Don't you see? We're winning!"

"Yes, that's wonderful."

"But it's not only that," Austin said, taking several papers out of his pocket. "It's what people are saying.

They are starting to understand that this war is justified, that it's necessary. Read these quotes."

He handed her a series of photocopied articles, with certain passages highlighted. She read the highlighted sections:

His point is well taken; religion is a force for evil in the world

He is right; a powerful, entrenched, intransigent religious power structure does exist; it is a force of oppression; and it cannot be reasoned with.

He has pointed out, with some degree of precision, the fact that religionists, while trying to tell us what to believe, do not agree amongst themselves about even the most basic, fundamental, and rudimentary ideas and doctrines that comprise their faith

He is forcing us to face the fact that organized religion, in a thousand subtle ways, does violence to people all the time. The powerful can disguise their violence; they can murder without breaking any laws; the rest of us can't. The powerbrokers of a religious culture responsible for the indoctrination, oppression, and death of thousands, do not face any risk of jail. But if the "War on Religion killer" is apprehended, he faces sure and swift justice. No doubt he is a madman, but, in a very real sense, he is also a martyr.

Sam handed him the papers back. "That's great," she said.

"Don't you see," Austin said. "We're winning!"

"I do see," she replied.

Her voice, however, was weak and her eyes blank. The truth was she didn't feel like a winner. Not one bit.

Chapter 27

Burt Witter smiled and introduced himself as Nick Gallo shook his hand. "Is there something I can help you with, sheriff?" he asked.

"Probably not," the sheriff replied, "but I'd like to talk with you, anyway."

"Sure," Nick said. "Come on in."

The sheriff came in, his sheriff's hat in his hand. He just stood there awkwardly, like a boy waiting for his prom date. "Have a seat," Nick said, motioning toward the sofa.

"Don't mind if I do," the sheriff said gratefully.

Nick thought he detected a slight accent. "Are you from down South by any chance?" he asked.

The sheriff smiled broadly, as if delighted that Nick noticed. "Why, yes," he said. "I'm originally from Alabama."

"Is that so?" Nick said.

"Sure is," the sheriff replied.

The two just sat there staring at each other for a moment. Then the sheriff cut to the chase. "I'm investigating a disappearance," he said. "Of a preacher."

He showed Nick a photo. "Have you ever seen this man?"

"I can't say that I have," Nick replied.

"I didn't think so," the sheriff said, then shook his head, as if dejected. He reminded Nick a little bit of Colombo. He had that same "Aw, shucks" sort of way about him, the same dumb-like-a-fox quality. "I guess I should tell you; I also questioned your sister about it."

"Yes, she told me," he said.

"Thing is," the sheriff said, "she was probably the last person to speak to Terrence."

"That is peculiar," he said.

"Yes," the sheriff said. He stopped and thought for a moment. "Tell me, what do you think of The War on Religion murders? I was thinking it's probably a former preacher. What do you think?"

Nick shrugged. "I really don't know. I think it's a strong possibility."

"I *was* thinking it was a former preacher," he said, "That's the profile the Feds came up with. But now, I'm starting to wonder if maybe we've all been barking up the wrong tree. I'm starting to wonder if maybe it's not a former preacher at all, but rather someone who is still in the ministry."

"Anything's possible," Nick said, disgusted at the mere thought. But then again, everything about these murders disgusted him.

"You don't know of any ministers who might be capable of such a thing, do you?" the sheriff asked. "You know, someone harboring a secret resentment? A grudge of some kind?"

"Well, I've met my share of ornery ministers," Nick offered. "But none come to mind that I believe are capable of such a thing."

"I didn't think so," the sheriff said, then put his hands on his knees and pushed himself up off of the sofa. "Well, time for me to be moseying on."

"Is that one of those Alabama expressions?" Nick joked.

The sheriff let out a hearty laugh and said, "I guess it is. I guess it is." The two men shook hands and the sheriff went on his way.

Nick stood by the door, watching him go.

Chapter 28

Nick found himself in a now familiar position: sitting by the bed of Martin Monroe, looking into the dead, gray eyes of the Thing that now resided in his body. "Okay, you win," he said. "You're going to get your trial."

"Excellent," the Thing said.

"I don't know what you think you will achieve."

"I just want my day in court. I want to be heard."

"And what about the lawyers, the judge, the jury?"

"What about them?"

"Who do you wish to prosecute God? Did you have anyone in mind?"

"I will leave it to you. I trust your sense of fair play."

"You're leaving it all up to me?"

"Yes."

"And you will abide by the results? No matter what?"

"Yes."

"What about the jury?"

"No jury," the Thing said.

"Don't you want a verdict," Nick asked, confused.

"Oh, yes," the Thing said. "There will be a verdict."

"How can there be a verdict with no jury?"

195

"The people will vote," the Thing said.

"The people?"

"Yes. The viewers will watch the trial, then, when the proceedings have ended, they will vote."

To his surprise, Nick actually liked that idea. "Okay," he said, "That's fair enough."

"That's very fair."

"People tend to side with God," Nick said. "It is an axiom that God is good, and most people simply accept it. The prosecutor will have a hard time getting a guilty verdict."

"I agree," the Thing said. "But not as hard as you think."

He smiled impishly as he spoke those last words.

"Very well, then. I will arrange everything," Nick said.

"You do that," the Thing answered.

With that, Nick left. He was relieved, but also wary. It all seemed too easy. Was a public rehashing of ancient theological quibbles, along with a verdict thrown in, really going to satisfy this Thing? And what made him so confident? It really did seem too easy. Nick had learned never to trust anything that seemed too easy.

Chapter 29

The buzz was on.

In the weeks since Nick had announced the trial, the press had taken a lively interest in the story. A nationally broadcast television program was going to put God on trial! And the viewers would decide His guilt or innocence! It was precisely the kind of story the press couldn't resist.

At first, the interest was moderate—confined mostly to the religious community. Religious broadcasters, both on TV and radio, had found something they could sink their teeth into. Panels of theologians convened for roundtable discussions; preachers thundered from the pulpit; religious columnists shared their viewpoints; and internet bloggers filled cyberspace with trenchant commentary and emotional opinions. And slowly, but surely, the buzz began to spread from the religious to the secular, until, by trial time, everyone was talking about it.

The panelists on political roundtables discussed the cultural ramifications. The morning talk show hosts wondered: Will God be found guilty? The evening news wondered: Have people given up on God?

Everyone had an opinion and everyone wondered: How will they conduct such a trial? Who will the attorneys be? What kind of evidence will be introduced? What will the charges be? What will the defense be? What about witnesses? Rules of evidence? And so on and so forth. To say there was plenty of grist for conversation would be an understatement.

Nick was surprised at all the commotion. Surprised, but not completely shocked. Somehow, it all seemed like part of a plan. All of the events of the past few months seemed connected — the Cockers murders, the War on Religion killings, the Martin Monroe situation. All of it seemed to be orchestrated by that Thing, and geared toward putting God on trial before the largest possible audience. And now, after all of the murder, mayhem, and misery, the Thing had what he wanted — a trial. His arch enemy would be investigated, His conduct challenged, His character examined, and His intentions scrutinized in such a way that the world would have an opportunity to reconsider their opinion of Him, and to announce, as one body, through an official verdict, exactly what they thought of Him. It was no wonder the press was having such a field day with the story. The verdict, whichever way it went, could have far-reaching implications; indeed, it could shape opinion for decades to come.

That, Nick supposed, was exactly how the Thing wanted it.

Chapter 30

It was the eve before the trial—The Trial of the Century, as the media dubbed it. It was also Super Bowl Sunday. And at halftime, as a nod to the impending trial, there would be a special performance. One hundred children's choirs, gleaned from churches around the nation, would perform together, on the field. They would be singing a song called "Sometimes There's God"—a non-denominational tome penned by John Mellencamp. Basically, the song asked some questions and expressed some thoughts that seemed to reflect the general mood of the world at the time. It was, perhaps, a prayer—a way for the world to say: We hope you're there, Lord; we hope you can hear us, and we hope you will help us. The children singing would be between the ages of eight and ten.

Nick smiled at Cassie, seated next to him on the couch. "Who's up for some popcorn?" Nick asked, getting up and strolling into the kitchen.

"Sounds great," Cassie said.

He returned with a big bowl of popcorn, topped off by some potato chips and pretzels.

"Ummm!" Cassie said, digging in. They turned their attention to the screen as the camera zoomed in on midfield, where the massive throng of children, arrayed in white robes, had assembled in formation. The music began, followed closely by a thousand angelic voices, filling the air of the huge stadium with a sweet, enchanting harmony.

"Oh, that's so lovely," Cassie said.

Nick did not respond.

"Right?" she said, nudging him.

"Oh...Um...yeah, it's very nice," Nick replied absently.

Something seemed wrong. He didn't know what. He hadn't even felt like watching the Super Bowl, but something had told him to watch. Something inside of him, but not really him. God? That thing? He didn't know. But as he watched he began to get a sick feeling. And then the smell. Faint at first, then stronger. He recognized it; it was unmistakable. It was the same smell that he had experienced when he was in the room with Martin. It was that Thing.

He looked at Cassie. Did she smell it? Did she feel it? Apparently not; she sat there casually munching away at the popcorn. As he watched the children, a wave of dread washed over him. He wanted to scream out to them. To warn them. And then, suddenly, everything slowed down and he was seeing in black and white. He watched helplessly as the children started to sink. A giant sinkhole had opened up on the field and was swallowing the children. It was happening fast, but to Nick, it seemed slow, as the scene unraveled inch by inch before him in vivid detail: the children's eyes widening in shock; their screams as they felt the ground giving in; their faces looking out at the crowd, for their mommies, as they sank; and finally, their little hands, stretching out, palms opened, as if waiting for someone to grab them, as they disappeared for good into the soil.

And then it was over. Nothing remained except a field with a huge hole in it. The crowd was frantic; people poured out of their seats in droves, screaming, running to the field. The commentators were aghast. "This can't be happening!" one kept saying. "Oh, my God," the other said over and over, as if no other words could even begin to express the horror of what had just transpired, on live TV, with the whole world watching. And suddenly, Nick flashed back to his conversation with the Thing:

The prosecutor will have a hard time getting a guilty verdict.

Not as hard as you think.

He recalled the Thing's impish smile as he spoke those words. Now he knew why it was so confident. It had a plan. It had caused this catastrophe. On the eve of the trial, it wanted to make God look guilty. No doubt it had succeeded in the minds of many. Of just how many only time would tell.

Nick gathered Cassie into his arms. She wept. "That Thing did this," he said.

She looked at him with a mixture of disbelief and horror. "How could anything want to kill a thousand children?" she asked.

Nick said nothing. He had felt that Thing's hatred. He knew how it could want to kill *anything*. He threw his arms around his wife as she wept.

Chapter 31
The Trial

The courtroom was packed. Filled to the rafters with reporters and interested observers, and flanked on all sides with cameras. Looking around from his seat at the defense table, Nick thought he had done a pretty good job. With some help from his producer, Todd, and a few others, he had pretty much arranged the whole thing. The county had been kind enough to lend them the courtroom for this event, helping to give the whole proceeding an extra air of authenticity. Nick had decided on the format, too: Basically, the trial would be a mix of a standard trial and a debate. He would serve as the defense attorney, defending God. The prosecuting attorney was Winston Barnett—one of the world's leading atheists, and the author of a bestselling book called *Christ is a Crock*.

They would follow the usual courtroom procedures: the prosecution would make its case first, call its witnesses, etc.... The defense would then have the opportunity to cross-examine. Then the defense would make its case, followed by cross-examination by the prosecution. Unlike a courtroom trial, however, the defense and prosecution attorneys would cross-examine each other. That's because Nick and Barnett were serving, in effect, as both attorneys *and* witnesses, for the prosecution and the defense, respectively; hence each man would have the opportunity to cross-examine the other. A real court judge, Roger Haley, agreed upon by both sides, would preside. And the viewers would serve as the jury.

The judge called the court to order, said a few introductory words, then said, "The prosecution will now give its opening statement."

Opening Statement for the Prosecution

Nick watched with admiration as Winston stood up and strolled confidently to the front of the room. Winston had presence. When he spoke, you could not help but listen. For 40 years, he had been one of the most eloquent and vocal voices of the Atheist movement. He was 72 years old, with a mop of wavy, white hair, and he walked with a slight limp due to an old injury. He wore slacks and a jacket, with patches on the elbows, like a hipster college professor, and a black hat, which, he liked to say, was only fitting for a man who so many regarded as an evil infidel. His glasses hung on a string around his neck. Nick was grateful the trial would not be decided on charisma, or he would have no chance.

As there was no jury in the courtroom, Winston simply looked into the camera and addressed the jury at home. "I would like to start off by thanking Nick and Cassie Gallo and the good folks at Sword of the Spirit Ministries for asking me to be a part of this proceeding."

He looked at Nick and Cassie, sitting together at the defense table, and nodded. Nick nodded back. Winston continued with his opening statement. "We are here, as you all know, to conduct a trial. It is not your ordinary trial. And it is not your ordinary defendant. The defendant, as you all know by now, is none other than God Himself. Yes, God. His infinite Majesty; Lord of the Universe; Father of Lights; Ruler of Heaven and Earth.... I'm sure you all know of whom it is I speak. It is that God, the God of Abraham, Isaac, and Jacob, who is on trial today. Unfortunately...."

He paused and ambled slowly over to the defense table, dragging his injured leg behind him, then continued, "Unfortunately...He is not here." He pointed to the defense table, where the defendant normally sits, and repeated, "That's right; the defendant is not here. So, barring a surprise appearance, we will be trying Him in absentia. The defendant is not here. I want you to think about that for a moment. Here He is, on trial for *criminal negligence*, for *neglecting* or *ignoring* us, and what does He do? Why, He doesn't show up for the trial, of course! Well, if I was the member of a jury, and the defendant did not show up for the trial, that would seal it for me. I would vote Guilty. That would do it for me. But...should we really be surprised? *Not being there* is what God does. He's never there! Now, as an atheist, I would suggest that He's never there because He doesn't exist. But for the purposes of this trial, we are assuming that He does exist. And so I must modify my position; He's never there, not because He doesn't exist; He's never there because *He doesn't care!*"

Winston paused again, then continued in a low, solemn voice: "But He does care, you say."

Another pause.

"You say He does, and I say He doesn't. And that's why we're here today. I am going to try to prove to you, beyond a reasonable doubt, that God simply doesn't care. And since this is a trial, I intend to call witnesses. Their testimony will prove, beyond a reasonable doubt, that God does not care about us and is guilty of the charge of criminal negligence."

With that, he thanked the court and sat down.

The judge thanked him for his statement and called for the defense to make theirs. Nick arose and strolled up to the front of the courtroom. He looked into the camera and began speaking.

Opening Statement for the Defense

"If anyone thinks the idea of putting God on trial is a novel one, I assure you it is not. It is at least several thousand years old. Most of you have heard of the book of Job. Well, Job was a man who suffered terribly. I daresay that Job probably suffered as much as anyone who ever lived. Indeed, if he were alive today I have no doubt that Mr. Barnett would have presented him as his star witness. That's because Job was forced to endure almost every manner of suffering known to man. He lost his oxen, asses, sheep, and camel. He lost his children. And he lost his health. The litany of physical afflictions he endured could have filled any emergency room. He experienced: boils, intense pain, peeling skin, emaciation, fever, depression, weeping, sleeplessness, nightmares, putrid breath, trouble breathing, failing vision, and intense itching. And to top it all off, his own wife abandoned him, telling him to 'curse God and die, already.'

"You probably know Job as a righteous man, one of the great biblical patriarchs of the Old Testament, and so, you may think his reaction to all of suffering was to grin and bear it, like a good Christian, or a good Jew, should. Well, if that's what you think, you'd be wrong. What was Job's response? Well, he got mad. Really mad. At God.

Among other things, he accused God of: Treating him like a sea monster, obsessing over him, as if he were a threat to Him, harassing him, creating him simply to torment him, expecting too much of him, treating him unjustly, behaving sadistically toward him, not understanding him, fencing him in and destroying him, and persecuting him.

"But not only that; he wanted to put God on trial. Job 23:3-5 says: O that I knew where I might find him! That I might come even to his seat! I would order my cause before him, and fill my mouth with arguments. I would know the words which he would answer me, and understand what he would say unto me.

"In other words: if I could just put Him on trial! But Job also realized there was a problem with putting God on trial. He touches on it in chapter 37, verse 19, saying: Teach us what we shall say to Him; we cannot arrange our case because of darkness.

"If anyone who ever lived had the right to try God, and find Him guilty, it was Job. And yet he realized he couldn't do it. Why? Because of the distance in wisdom between himself and God. He simply did not have sufficient information to convict God.

"That was three thousand years ago, but I would like to suggest that his words are just as true today as they were when they were written. It is a fact that water cannot rise above its source. For this reason it is impossible for man to convict God. If He were evil, He would be a better criminal that we would be detectives; hence, we could not gather sufficient evidence against Him. We are in no position to argue with God. It is simply not possible, and I would like to suggest that we all know it. Consider: Who really tries to make the case that God is evil? Practically no-one. They may say He doesn't *exist*, but they almost never try to convince us that He's evil. Why? Because they know that such a contention simply won't fly. If God *is*, then the only appropriate response is to bow down before Him as Lord of the Universe."

Witnesses for the Prosecution

Next the judge called for the Prosecution to call its witnesses. Winston strolled up to the front of the courtroom and said: "I would like to call my first witness: Mr. Abraham Schwartz."

Nick watched somberly as an elderly man, bald and hunched over, hobbled slowly to the witness stand, and sat down. The man's testimony was compelling, and Winston, old fox that he was, left no stone unturned as he helped the man recount the nightmare of Auschwitz one gory detail at a time. Among the details recounted: Being torn away from his family as a child, being stuffed, naked, into box cars for transport, with barely room enough to move; being forced into the prison camps; toiling 16 hours a day; having almost nothing to eat; watching those around him die slow, agonizing deaths; watching hordes being marched off to the gas chamber to die; and watching as his once robust body shriveled away to skin and bones.

He spoke slowly, haltingly, his tone grave; his voice labored and deliberate. When he was finished, Winston asked: "Tell me, Mr. Schwartz: When you were first taken by the Nazis, were you religious?"

"Yes, I was. Very. My whole family."

"How did you and your family express your religion?"

"We went to temple. We prayed. We observed all the rules of our faith. My parents were known throughout our neighborhood for always helping anybody in need. My father would never turn someone away."

"And what happened to your father, Mr. Schwartz?"

"He was killed in the gas chamber. My mother, too. And my five brothers and sisters. And all my relatives. I'm the only one who survived."

At this point, Winston paused for a good bit, before asking:

"Do you still believe in God, Mr. Schwartz?"

Abraham thought about it for a minute, then said, in a halting voice that crackled with sadness: "Yes, but I...no longer think...He believes in me."

On that note, Winston excused the witness.

There were more.

In fact, he was just getting started. All told, he called a total of ten witnesses. Each had a worse tale to tell than the last. A nurse who lost her husband and two children in a car wreck. A single mother who lost her only two children to cancer. A social worker who was gang-raped and held hostage for ten hours by the very people she was trying to help. A man who watched his wife and daughter raped and killed in a home invasion. A mother whose nine-year-old girl was abducted, raped, then buried alive.

And so on.

In each instance Winston stressed several factors: First, that the victim had done nothing to deserve their fate. Second, that the horrors endured served no ostensible purpose, either in molding the person's own character, or in helping those around them. And third, that God could have prevented it, and didn't.

After excusing the last witness, he again addressed the jury, saying: "The law defines Criminal Negligence as: recklessly acting without reasonable caution and putting another person at risk of injury or death (or failing to do something with the same consequences). What is needed to prove negligence under the law? Three things: That the person charged had the opportunity to prevent the harm in question, that he had the ability, and that he had the responsibility to do so. In each of the cases we just examined, grave harm came to someone. I would submit that in every one of these cases, our three criterions are easily met. In every case, God had the ability to prevent the harm in question, He had the opportunity, and He had the responsibility. And yet, in each and every case, He failed to act. That, according to the law, is criminal negligence."

On that note, he rested his case and went back to his seat at the prosecution table.

Cross-Examination for the Defense

Now came the cross-examination. For obvious reasons, Nick declined to cross-examine the witnesses, and instead went right for Winston. The judge had Winston sit in the witness box for this portion of the proceeding.

Nick approached Winston tentatively, like an animal approaching a dangerous prey. "Mr. Barnett," he said. "It seems to me that the thrust of your argument with regard to these witnesses is this: God allowed more harm to come to them than He should have. Is that correct?"

"Yes," Winston replied.

"Well, then, let me ask you this. How much harm is permissible for God to allow to occur to a particular individual in their lifetime? And please be as specific as possible."

"I don't know," Winston replied. He did not seem disturbed by his inability to answer the question.

"Well, then," Nick pressed, "let me see if I understand this. You don't know how much harm a good God might allow to befall a person, and yet you have accused Him of allowing too much harm in the cases you presented. Is that correct?"

"That is entirely correct," Winston replied confidently.

"Please explain how you can accuse God of crossing a line when you yourself do not know where that line ought to be drawn?" Nick said.

"We do it all the time," Winston replied. "I'll give you an example. We all agree that a man has the right to discipline his child. Some of us might even be strong proponents of corporeal punishment. But can we draw a sharp, crystal clear line as to when a man has crossed over from discipline to abuse; from spanking to beating? I think not. What constituted a spanking in my generation—and I received my fair share—would be considered child abuse these days. And yet we can all agree that in certain cases the line has been crossed—in the case, for instance, of a child who suffers severe blunt force trauma to the head. And so, contrary to your assertion, we need not know precisely where a line begins to know when it has been crossed."

"Excellent point, Mr. Barnett," Nick said, undeterred by the elder man's strong response. "But tell me this: In the case of child abuse, do we have at least an *idea* of where that line might begin?"

"I believe so," Winston replied.

"I quite agree," Nick said. "So again, I ask you: In the case of God, can you tell me at least *approximately* how much suffering is permissible for Him to allow in the case of a particular individual?"

"As you know, suffering cannot be quantified, as in

the case of tangible objects, such as apples or widgets, but generally speaking, I would say in response to your question: As much as is necessary to correct and educate the person who is suffering."

"You are quite correct; suffering cannot be quantified. Nor can the positive effects it might produce. How can we know, then, that the sum total of suffering in the world, is not, in some way not apparent to us, producing an overall positive effect that outweighs the negative?"

"I suppose we cannot know it. But I think it is reasonably inferred from the evidence."

"Evidence we can measure only from our own vantage point, which, all would agree, is extremely limited when compared with God's."

"If you can tell me what good could *possibly* come from the slow, agonizing death of a child from cancer, or a prisoner in a Nazi war camp, I am all ears, Mr. Gallo."

"I would like to suggest that if we could actually see the likely positive results of every instance of suffering in the world, then that suffering would assume a radically different character, so much so that it would almost cease to be true suffering. And I do not believe it is unreasonable to believe that God wished for there to be at least some true suffering in this world. Why must suffering exist? Perhaps because, in the very nature of things, there is no other path to the highest good. Perhaps that is why God Himself chose to reveal Himself as a man of sorrows. Perhaps *He* is the answer to the question of suffering."

"Perhaps," Winston said. "But I do not think it is probable, especially since He chose to give a different answer to most of the world's population, who never even heard of Him. You talk about the good outweighing the bad in the long run. But if your belief regarding hell is true, I don't see how the good can outweigh the bad for the vast majority of people who are consigned to suffer endless torment in hell."

"Perhaps it can't if you confine God's plans merely to our own race. But perhaps we are only one of millions of races meant to eventually populate God's Kingdom. Perhaps He has set us forth as an example for these other races, that they might see in God's dealings with us the full measure of His wrath in punishing sin."

"That is very nice for the other races, but probably of little comfort to the billions of souls who will spend all eternity roasting in a red, hot flame. It is also extremely hypothetical and far-fetched. It seems that whenever the Christian Religious system is backed into a corner, it either pleads mystery or retreats into outlandish hypothetical scenarios. I, on the other hand, am trying to deal in facts, and the ones I have presented here today are more than enough to convict God of the charge in question."

Feeling that he made his point, Nick turned to the judge and said, "I have no further questions." Winston and Nick returned to their seats at their respective tables, where Nick proceeded to prepare to give his opening statement. Moments later, he stood up, strolled up to the front of the courtroom, and addressed the jury.

The Case for the Defense

Having no witnesses, Nick dived right into his statement.

"I cannot explain, or even justify, all of the pain in the world. I will, however, put forth three propositions which, I believe, might help to make sense of the existence of pain.

"Number one is this: It is probable that in the best of all worlds, which, of course, is the one God would create, there would exist at least some measure of pain. I do not think this is controversial. Simply consider the alternative: A universe where everyone exists in a state of absolute perfection from their very inception. Perfect in knowledge. Perfect in wisdom. Perfect in might. Perfect in character. Perfectly happy. Sprung from the womb of creation as a perfect, complete, finished product, without a thing to learn or an obstacle to overcome, perhaps quivering with pleasure.

"Is such a universe likely? Or even desirable? A universe where every single created being exists eternally in a state of static bliss? With no room for development? No room for learning? No characters to be molded? No facts to be learned? No mountains to climb? Maybe such a universe is the best one possible; I don't know. But I do know this: I don't think it is a stretch to say that it probably isn't. And as soon as we admit this, then we have conceded that a world which includes suffering is not an indictment of God.

"This brings me to my second proposition. As soon as we allow for some suffering, the question then turns to the kind of suffering, and the amount. And this brings me back to my earlier point—my point about the character of pain. Yes, much pain in the world seems pointless, random, and cruel in character. But how could pain exist any other way? Are we really going to propose a world in which pain exists, but every instance of it yields immediate, quantifiable positive results? That would not be pain at all.

"And that leads me to my third proposition. Any amount of pain will seem like too much to us. Think about it. To a small child, the smallest inconvenience, the tiniest intrusion into his comfortable world, seems utterly unbearable. Gradually, however, our pain threshold increases, until, as adults, we can endure pain and distress in quantities which we could have never endured as children. Pain is never welcomed. It is always resisted. And at any given stage of development, it seems like too much—like more than we could bear, like more than we should *have* to bear.

"And yet bear it we do. And gradually, in stages, over many years, we grow stronger. We can bear more and more of it. And who do we bear it for? Our children, who still can bear it only in small doses. And at a certain point, we even begin to welcome a certain amount of pain, of sacrifice, of toil, because we know that they produce certain rewards. Our relationship to suffering begins to change as we mature. We begin to see a kind of latent pleasure in pain. Sacrifice brings rewards. The more mature we become, the stronger we become, the more suffering we can endure, and the more we are willing to embrace suffering. And again, this is where the example of Christ is instructive, for He, as the model human, was defined chiefly by His willingness to suffer.

"But I do not wish to delve too deeply into this matter; it is beyond the purview of this discussion. For our purposes, here today, I only wish to suggest three things: One, the existence of suffering provides no grounds for indicting God, and, when understood, may even provide evidence of His ambitious plans for mankind, for it is our capacity for suffering that lends meaning to our existence; Two: The suffering in question must be real suffering, and, as such, there must not always be an obvious and immediate correlation between suffering and rewards;

and Three: Any amount of suffering will always seem like too much; hence the quantity of suffering in the world is not sufficient grounds to convict God.

"In closing, let me say simply that the prosecution has failed to make its case. It has proposed that the existence, character, and quantity of pain in the world serve as grounds to convict God of negligence. I maintain that the evidence shows no such thing."

Nick sat back down, exchanged smiles with Cassie, and waited for the judge to announce the next phase of the proceedings—the cross-examination. The judge promptly asked the Prosecution if it wished to cross-examine. It accepted, and Nick stood up and strolled over to the witness box and took a seat. He watched as Winston approached, slowly, like a wolf measuring its prey.

Cross Examination for the Prosecution

"So, God didn't want things perfect from the start. Is that your contention, Mr. Gallo?"

"Yes," Nick replied.

"Doesn't that contradict two thousand years of orthodox Christian tradition which states, quite emphatically, that God did create everything perfect, and that imperfection came about through an *unwanted* transgression on the part of man?"

"Yes, I suppose it does," Nick said.

"And as a pastor, are you not part of that tradition?"

"Yes, I suppose that I am."

"So, in order to defend God, and explain suffering, you are contradicting your own religious tradition, are you not?"

"I am proposing one possibility."

"Not just a possibility. You presented it as a

probability, did you not?"

"Yes, I did."

"And it does contradict Christian tradition, correct?"

"There are a number of schools of thought with regard to the matter of man's original perfection; the Christian system does not speak with one voice with regard to this."

"Of course it doesn't. It all depends on what point it is trying to prove, doesn't it? When it wishes to defend the doctrine of eternal torment, it insists on man's original perfection. After all, it would be cruel to make man imperfect, then punish him forever for the sins that spring naturally from that imperfection. In that tradition, the existence of sin is a mystery. But today, your goal is not to indict man; it is to propose a reason for suffering; hence you shift shape, as Christians always do, and declare that God made us imperfect and that sin and suffering, far from being mysterious, are merely what you would expect from a perfect Creator. Have I presented the case accurately?"

Boxed into a corner, Nick simply said, "I suppose you have."

"Then your explanations, your defense of God, are not really rooted in Christian thinking. They are simply ad hoc arguments patched together in desperation in order to defend an obviously guilty defendant, are they not?"

"I would not go that far," Nick said.

"Well, you *did* go that far, Mr. Gallo, and it's very sad that you did. I have no further questions."

Cassie's Testimony

With that, the two men returned to their respective tables. As Nick prepared for the closing statements part of the proceedings, Cassie, to his surprise, stood up and addressed the judge. "Your honor," she said, "may I say a few words." The judge agreed, and Cassie strolled up to the front of the courtroom.

Nick watched with interest as his wife prepared to speak. He had never seen her look so solemn. She stood there, silently, for a long time, and for a moment Nick thought she had forgotten what she wanted to say. Then finally she spoke, her words slow and measured, and bereft of the usual cheer that had always infused her speech in the past.

"I would like to begin on a personal note," she said. "Six years ago my son died."

If Nick was surprised before, he was even more surprised now. This was something Cassie never spoke about, and he was amazed she would choose to do so here, in front of millions. Even so, he knew where she was going with it, and it deepened his admiration for her. That she was willing to do this in order to defend God revealed the true depths of her devotion.

"Everyone thought he died of an accidental overdose of prescription pills," she said. That was the official story. She paused and took a deep breath. "But that's not true," she continued. "He killed himself."

Nick's eyes widened with surprise. He could not believe what he was hearing.

"He killed himself...because he was gay."

You could hear a pin drop in the courtroom as she continued. "He was gay and we never told anyone, never reached out for help. All we did was pray for him and try to change him, so that God wouldn't have to torture him forever in hell. But God didn't answer our prayers. Raymond stayed gay. He lived gay and he died gay. But he spent his whole short life trying to be two people. The person he was and the person he wanted — we wanted — him to be. And no-one can be two people.

"But I'm not up here to blame God, and I'm not up here to defend Him, either. The truth is: God shouldn't be on trial at all. That's a waste of time. If God exists, then He's God and that's it. It's not about Him. It's about us. It's about the God we're willing to worship. Mr. Barnett is right: My husband presented a defense here today that is not in keeping with Christian tradition. And that's because Christianity can't make up his mind. And that's because it is not honest. Tell the truth and it's easy to keep your facts straight, and to stick to one set of them. But lie, even to yourself, and it becomes difficult. And when it comes to religion, I see a lot of lying. To each other and to ourselves."

She took a piece of paper out of her pocket and said, "I would like to read you a quote."

"*But as men farther exalt their idea of divinity, it is their notion of his power and knowledge only, not of his goodness, which is improved. On the contrary, in proportion to the supposed extent of his science and authority, their terrors naturally augment; while they believe, that no secrecy can conceal them from his scrutiny, and that even the inmost recesses of their breast lie open before him. They must then be careful not to form expressly any sentiment of blame and disapprobation. All must be applause, ravishment, ecstasy. And while their gloomy apprehensions make them ascribe to him measures of conduct, which, in human creatures, would be highly blamed, they must still affect to praise and admire that conduct in the object of their devotional addresses. Thus it may be safely affirmed, that popular religions are really, in the conception of their more vulgar votaries, a species of demonism; and the higher the deity is exalted in power and knowledge, the lower of course is he depressed in goodness and benevolence;*

whatever epithets of praise may be bestowed upon him by his amazed followers. Among idolaters, the words may be false, and belie the secret opinion. But among more secret religionists, the opinion itself contracts a kind of falsehood, and belies the inward sentiment. The heart secretly detests such measures of cruel and implacable vengeance; but the judgment dares not but pronounce them perfect and adorable. And the additional misery of this inward struggle aggravates all the other terrors, by which these unhappy victims to superstition are forever haunted."[iii]

Cassie folded up the paper and put it back in her pocket. She took a deep breath, the resumed speaking.

"Maybe we don't have to decide if God is *good* or if He's *bad*. Maybe we have a right to be angry at Him sometimes. And if He's God, then He understands that, and we don't have to deny it, repress it, tell ourselves lies.

"So, how should you, the jury, vote? I don't know. And I don't think it matters. Maybe we can vote guilty and still believe, in the end, God will make things right. And maybe we can vote Not Guilty and still believe, in some way, that God is doing us a temporary injustice. I don't know. I really don't. But I do know this: anyone who can watch a thousand children swallowed alive by a field of hungry dirt and not be angry at God is sick.

"And I don't think that repressing that anger is the answer. Maybe those kids, when they were singing that song 'Sometimes There's God,' had the right idea. Maybe, for most of us, most of the time, that's the best we can do; that's the strongest confession we can make. And maybe that's okay with God; maybe He understands. If He made us, if He loves us, then it *has* to be okay."

She paused and took a deep breath. "Those children never got to finish their song. So today, in their honor, I would like to finish it for them." She read from a paper:

Sometimes there's God, in someone else's eyes,
Sometimes there's God, when you see the sunrise
Sometimes you work, only in vain
Sometimes there's God, in someone else's eyes,
Sometimes there's God, when you see the sunrise
Sometimes you work, only in vain
Sometimes there's very little heartbreak and pain
Sometimes there's God, Sometimes he's not
Sometimes there's God, Sometimes it just not

A little redemption would help us a lot
Sometimes there's God in the palm of your hand
Some days our crimes will cover your land
Sometimes there's God, Sometimes there's God
Sometimes there's God, sometimes there's just not

Sometimes you pray for a witness you can rise above
There's judgment and destruction in the name of God.
Can we find truth in all that we feel?
Sometimes there's God when sickness is healed
Sometimes there's God, Sometimes there's God
Sometimes there's God, sometimes there's not

We only got when people don't care
What we do to each other when there's nobody else there
In the dark we promise "God, we'll never do this again."
Let the choices we made, people give in
Sometimes there's God, Sometimes there's God
Sometimes there's God, Sometimes there's not

She folded the paper up and wiped a tear from her eye.

Nick watched, stunned, as she continued: "So, my final word to everyone is this. Love God when you can.

Hate Him when you must. He's a big boy; He can take it. How we treat each other is more important than how we treat Him. The Bible tells us: You cannot love God, who you cannot see, and hate man, who you can see. So love the people you can see. Show your love for God that way.

"And finally, know that your preachers and teachers, whoever they are, or wherever they're from, are just people, like you and me. They are fallible; they don't have a monopoly on the truth. If they did, they would not all disagree with each other. They have no right to tell you to fly a plane into a building, or to hate gays, or to shoot abortion doctors, or how to vote, or anything else. Think for yourselves. Do what you think is right, and if it's wrong, then it's wrong. You will survive. But if you do what other people tell you to do, simply because they tell you to do it, then you will regret it. Take it from me; I know."

And with that she stood up and strolled back to the defense table.

Nick could not bring himself to make eye contact with her as she took her seat beside him. He did not know what to think. He was stunned. How could she air their laundry in public like that? Why didn't she discuss it with him first? At least give him a clue?

To make matters worse, he had no time to process what had just transpired. His head was spinning just as he had to make a closing statement before a world-wide audience. Moreover, her words made the entire endeavor seem trivial and immature. As he looked down at the speech he had prepared, the words suddenly seemed meaningless—just part of a rote, empty, academic exercise.

Fortunately, the judge called for a brief recess. Nick

just sat there, trying to gather his thoughts, to make sense of what had just happened. When he looked over at Cassie, she just said, "I'm sorry, Nick. I hope you understand."

But he didn't understand. Not at all. Suddenly, nothing made sense. Not his wife; not their relationship; not this trial; not even himself. What the hell was he doing here? Did he really believe all of this stuff? He didn't know. All he knew was that her words seemed to jog something loose in his brain. Suddenly, as he sat there trying to compose himself, he started remembering.

He was still reeling when the judge reconvened the proceedings. He needed more time to regroup, so he asked the judge if perhaps Winston could go first. The judge consented and Winston Barnett approached the front of the courtroom to give his closing statement.

Prosecution Closing Statement

"The Prosecution referenced me in his closing statement," he said, "if memory serves: They may say He doesn't *exist*, but they almost never try to convince us that He's evil. He's quite correct on this point; I have never said God is evil. I say He doesn't exist. But what's the difference? To say He doesn't exist is to say, in effect, that even if He does exist, He acts as if He doesn't, and isn't this tantamount to the charge in question — namely, criminal negligence?

"Let me put it this way: I can't prove to you that God doesn't exist. But I can prove the God we worship doesn't. I can prove to you that if He does exist, then He exists as a being who is entirely beyond human comprehension, for all attempts to comprehend Him have resulted in a fantastic farce of schism, lies, war, and fantastic theories, most of which cannot be true if the others are true. I can prove to you that if He exists, He exists as a God who's utterly beyond the reach of man, and man's theories, and yes, man's *defenses* for God. I can prove to you that we have no reason to trust in any of the defenses man offers for God, for they contradict each other at every turn. The prosecution says if God exists He is a God who cannot be convicted by man. But I say: If God exists, He is a God who cannot be *defended* by man. And so what are we left with? Only the evidence. The *facts*. And I have given you facts. Eyewitness testimony. The defense has not, for they have none to give!

"I can prove to you, beyond a reasonable doubt, that if God exists, He is not any of the Gods we worship; rather He is a God who behaves exactly as if He doesn't exist. He is a God who *may* care, but acts as if He doesn't. He is a God who *may* answer prayer, but acts as if He doesn't. He is a God who *may* wish to give us a clear, unambiguous revelation, but acts as if He doesn't. He is a God who *may* desire all men to be saved, but acts as if He doesn't. He is a God who wishes us to believe He made the world in six days, yet gives us overwhelming scientific evidence that the universe has existed for fifteen billion years.

"Let me make this as clear as I know how: The only God whose existence I cannot disprove is the one who disguises his every move as something else.

"All others—the gods who accurately predict the future, who actually answer prayer, who can be perceived objectively in any way, who write perfect books, who deliver on their promises—these Gods are easily disproven, just as I can disprove the existence of the Eiffel Tower in my backyard. That Eiffel Tower doesn't exist. There may be another one; I don't know, I can't prove it....

But the one in my backyard, I'm sure of it. It's not there.

"Again: The only God whose existence I can't disprove is the one who disguises his every move as something else. iv

"We live in a religiously ambiguous world. One that is consistent with God's existence and consistent with His non-existence. It is even consistent with the existence of an evil, or indifferent, or simply impotent God. The one thing it is not consistent with, based on the evidence, is a God of infinite might, wisdom, and benevolence. *This* God — the God of Religion — almost certainly does not exist. And if this God does exist, we're in no position to know Him. We're in no position to convict Him, and we're in no position to *defend* Him. All we can do is believe the only thing He has left us — the concrete, tangible, observable facts of our own five senses. So let us decide based on these facts, for even if God exists, He has left us nothing to judge Him by except these facts. And I'll say I once again: I have given you facts today. Eyewitness testimony. Evidence. And that is what we use to determine guilt or innocence. So all I ask of you, the jury, is that you believe your own eyes, and then vote accordingly. Thank you for your time and attention. I know you will make the right decision."

Winston Barnett checked the time on his time piece, and then slowly, and with a solemn expression, strolled back to his seat at the Prosecution table.

Closing Statement for the Defense

It was Nick's turn. As he approached the front of the courtroom, his mind bubbled with responses to Winston's arguments — responses he believed were philosophically sound, perhaps even unassailable. And yet they did not seem to matter. A personal incident, with clear theological implications, had just unfolded in a way that undercut his position and deflected attention away from the sterile arguments of the trial and onto the more titillating emotional drama of his own life and ministry. He felt it really was no longer God on trial, but him. How could he simply redirect the attention back onto God, as if nothing had happened? He couldn't, of course. He had to address it.

He stood before the courtroom preparing to speak. He stood there for a long time, trying to collect his thoughts, to marshal the right words, but none came. Instead, the words of his wife flashed through his mind: *he spent his whole short life trying to be who we wanted him to be. But that wasn't him. And no-one can be two people.*

Two people. Two people. Two...People. T-W-O...P-E-O-P-L-E.

The room was spinning, now; the faces blurry, like images from a dream. His heart was racing and he started to sweat. Something was wrong. Desperately wrong. Suddenly, Nick did not know who he was. He knew where he was; he recognized the faces in the seats; he knew his wife; he knew his name. But he didn't know who he was.

"Is everything okay?" the judge asked.

"Yes," Nick said instinctively, not because he was okay, but because that's what you say when people asked that question. But something very strange was happening to him. He was understanding who he was.

From her seat at the defense table, Cassie started to look concerned. "Nick?" she called out.

But he didn't answer. He just kept staring, blankly, into the cameras, as images began flooding his mind. He closed his eyes, trying to stop them, but they came anyway, like water rushing through a damn that was busting at the seams. The images were horrible. Images of a man being bound and gagged and thrown into the trunk of a car. Images of a man thrashing around on the floor, screaming in pain, as the room filled with searing heat. Images of a badly burned body being dumped into a pond. Images of blood and burns and torture and screams of agony. These images hit him with the force of a hammer, and he found himself sagging slowly to his knees, like a boxer after absorbing a solid combination. He put his head in his hands and began to sob.

Cassie rushed to his side, throwing her arms around him. Winston went over as well, and put a hand on Nick's shoulder. "Nick, it's okay," Cassie whispered, trying to comfort him. But he would not be comforted. He just kept crying, his whole body shaking from the sobs.

Several minutes passed. He stood up slowly. Cassie put a hand under his arm and led him back to the defense table. Nick folded his arms on the table and buried his face in them, like a child at recess in school. He did not want to look at anyone. When his sobs subsided, the judge called for a recess, ordering the two attorneys to join him in his chambers. Once there, he asked Nick if he would still like to make a closing statement. Nick declined. He saw no point in it. The court was reconvened and the judge addressed the audience, saying: "The defense and prosecution have finished presenting their cases. The only thing left now is to wait for the verdict. As you know, the people are deciding this case. As we speak the viewers are voting. In a few minutes we will announce the result."

A few minutes passed, and the judge said: "Ladies and gentleman, we have a verdict in the case of the people vs. God. On the count of criminal negligence the jury finds God.... Not Guilty."

And just like that, it was over. Nick did not feel like a winner. In fact, the trial already seemed like a distant memory—distant and small and utterly insignificant. The whole thing seemed like a childish game—a silly diversion from reality. And now he would have to face a whole new reality. He would have to tell Cassie what he had done. He would have to turn himself in. He would have to abandon the ministry. And he would probably have to spend the rest of his life in jail.

And that was what occupied his mind as he gathered his papers in his briefcase and prepared to exit the courtroom. The throng of reporters had already filed out; no doubt they were waiting outside for him and Winston to appear, where they would each make statement, and then answer questions. He looked over at Cassie. She took his hand in hers and kissed him on the cheek. They said nothing as they strolled down the aisle, toward the large, double doors leading out of the courtroom.

Epilogue

And They All Lived Happily Ever After

The first thing Nick did after the trial was sleep. He slept for fourteen hours straight. It was not a pleasant sleep. He had bad dreams. Horrible dreams. Dreams of the things he had done. The abductions. The torture. The murders. He tossed and turned all night, and woke up as tired as when he went to sleep.

Then he sat Cassie down and told her everything. It was the hardest thing he ever had to do. She reacted as anyone would under the circumstances. With disbelief. With shock. With tears. Rivers and rivers of tears.

The next thing he did was call Sam to tell her he was turning himself in, but she did not answer the phone.

Lastly, he drove to the police station, walked up to the front desk, and issued perhaps the most startling confession in the history of the criminal justice system. The War on Religion murderer was a church pastor.

For the trial Nick retained a world renowned expert in split personality disorders, and pleaded insanity. The defense was as simple as it was bizarre: In his effort to be the man he wanted to be, Nick had repressed his hatred of his father, of religion, and of God Himself. So effective was this repression that he essentially became two different persons—a church pastor and a serial killer. Neither of those persons admitted of the existence of the other, and each functioned as separate, distinct individuals. To the surprise of many, the jury bought it. They voted not guilty by reason of insanity. Nick was committed to a mental institution. He spent a full year there until he was cured.

During his stay he realized that there had in fact been no supernatural component to any of the events that had transpired. He had hallucinated those elements, including the seemingly supernatural components of his encounters with Martin Monroe. The two of them, he gradually realized, were not connected by the same demon. But there was a connection, he believed. What was it? Why did Martin seek him out? What was the true source of their connection? He did not know for sure, but one possible explanation did occur to him. In Scripture Satan is called the Prince of the Power of the Air. What travels through the air? Sounds. Waves. Radio waves. Radio waves are picked up by frequencies. Perhaps so are thoughts, Nick had speculated. You can absorb a song that's being played in the background, even if you don't know it's being played; you may even find yourself humming the song. Perhaps it was the same with thoughts. Maybe if you're on the same frequency as a person, their thoughts get through.

Upon his release, he moved back into his home with Cassie. Together they started a new ministry. He called it the *First Church of the Real Christ*, and it was substantively different from his earlier ministry. For one, he rejected the dogma of the inerrancy of Scripture, citing Christ Himself as an example, for He said: Your law says, but *I* say to you, thus drawing a distinction between what He believed and what scripture taught. He also insisted certain scriptures were given due to "the hardness of your hearts."

Nick also rejected a number of other cherished church teachings, such as man's original perfection, the satisfaction theory of the Atonement, and the doctrine of eternal torment. As a result of his new theological stance, Nick was ostracized from the evangelical conservative community, but that was okay with him; he found a new home among the more liberal minded, and his new ministry thrived.

He still visited Martin Monroe from time to time. Gradually, he got to know him and to like him. Eventually, Martin came to realize he was not possessed, and became more receptive to conventional treatments. They did not cure him, but they did help a lot. Eventually he was able to leave Riverview, moving into a halfway house for people with mental illnesses.

****

Cassie broke off her affair with Adam and re-devoted herself to her husband, who now, for the first time, was free of the past—free to be himself. And Cassie liked who he was underneath all of that baggage. This time, however, she did join him in his ministry. Instead, she decided to become an author, writing a book about their experience called *The Dark Side*, which sold over three million copies.

****

Adam continues to practice psychiatry at *Riverview*. Cassie's book proved a boon for his career, and he wrote one of his own: *The Easy Fix*, about people's inclination to attach supernatural meaning to the mundane events of life. He drew heavily on the Monroe case for the book.

****

As she began to read the writing on the wall, Sam gathered her belongings, hopped in her car, pointed it south, and did not look back. She now resides in Cancun, where she works nights as a waitress and spends her days at the beach. She calls Nick occasionally, just to talk and let him know she's okay.

Before You Go...

HELP AN AUTHOR

write a review

THANK YOU!

Share your voice and help guide other readers to these wonderful books. Even if it's only a line or two your reviews help readers discover the author's books so they can continue creating stories that you'll love. Login to your favorite retailer and leave a review. Thank you.

About the Author

I live and work in Toms River, NJ. I am the Christian Apologetics Examiner for the Examiner.com, which is a popular online publication that features on a wide array of topics. I also have published a book with wipf and Stock Publishers called *The Calvinist Universalist*, which has generated some rave reviews on Amazon, and I have a website that goes by the same name.
http://www.thecalvinistuniversalist.com/

I am married, with a seven year old boy.

---

[i] Essay entitled "From the Outside by Richard Smith 2013-10-6
[ii] Essay entitled "Christian Salvation", by Stephen Matthies 2002-02-27
[iii] David Hume, The History of Natural Religion, The Portable Atheist
[iv] God Doesn't Exist, You Say? … Which One? Peter Bradford Martin 9/28/2014 http://www.peterbradfordmartin.com/blog/2014/9/28

Made in the USA
Middletown, DE
25 July 2017